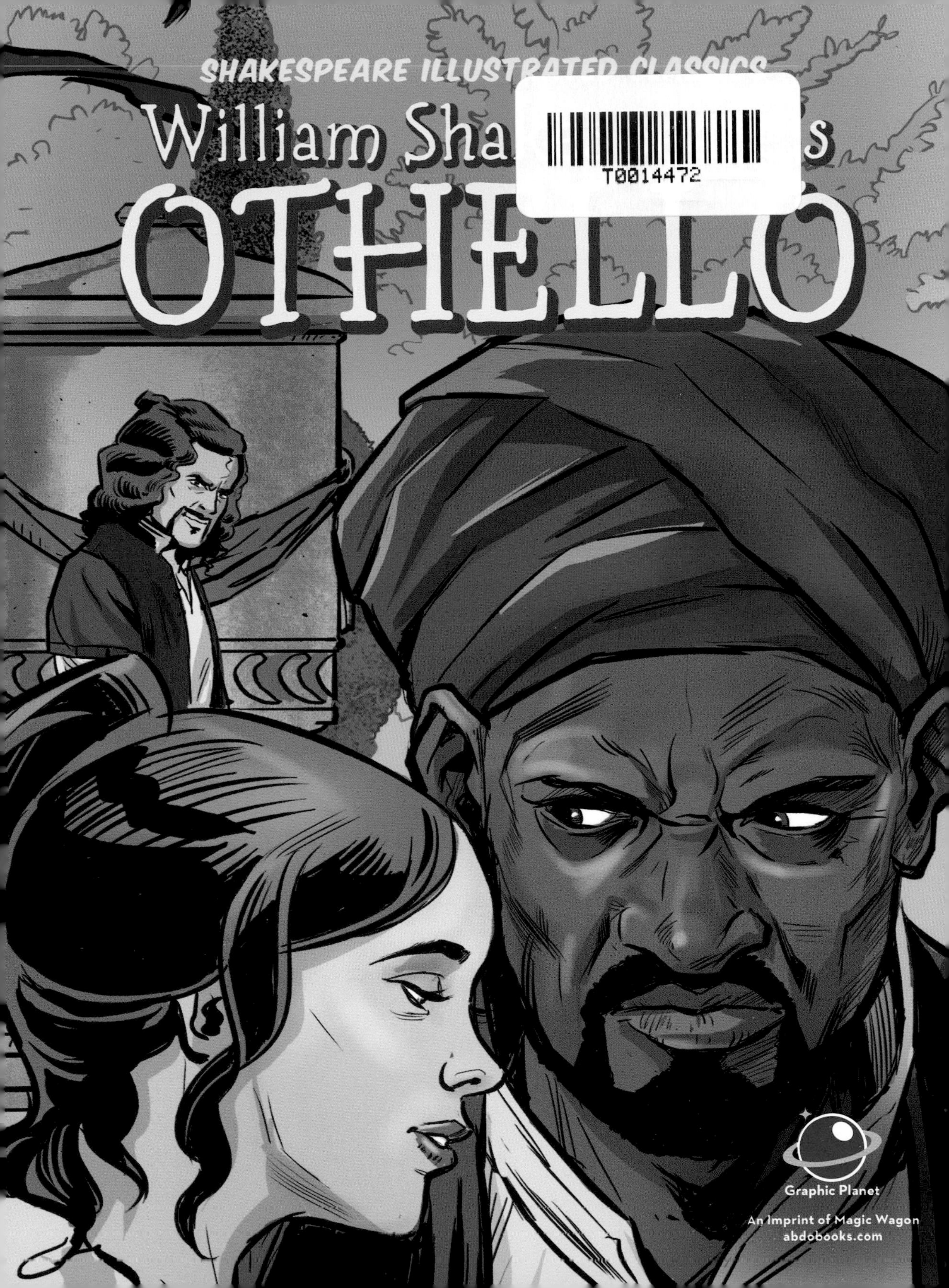
SHAKESPEARE ILLUSTRATED CLASSICS
William Sha s
OTHELLO
T0014472
Graphic Planet
An Imprint of Magic Wagon
abdobooks.com

abdobooks.com

Published by Magic Wagon, a division of ABDO, PO Box 398166, Minneapolis, Minnesota 55439. Copyright © 2023 by Abdo Consulting Group, Inc. International copyrights reserved in all countries. No part of this book may be reproduced in any form without written permission from the publisher. Graphic Planet™ is a trademark and logo of Magic Wagon.

Printed in the United States of America, North Mankato, Minnesota.
052022
092022

Adapted by Vincent Goodwin
Cover art by Dave Shephard
Interior art by Chris Allen
Edited by Tamara L. Britton
Interior layout and design by Candice Keimig and Colleen McLaren

Library of Congress Control Number: 2021951990

Publisher's Cataloging-in-Publication Data

Names: Shakespeare, William; Goodwin, Vincent, authors. | Allen, Chris, illustrator.
Title: William Shakespeare's Othello / by William Shakespeare, Adapted by Vincent Goodwin; illustrated by Chris Allen.
Description: Minneapolis, Minnesota: Magic Wagon, 2023. | Series: Shakespeare illustrated classics
Summary: Iago is mad when his general, Othello, denies him a promotion, so he manipulates Othello into believing his wife is unfaithful, with tragic results.
Identifiers: ISBN 9781098233310 (lib. bdg.) | ISBN 9781644948453 (pbk.) | ISBN 9781098234157 (ebook) | ISBN 9781098234577 (Read-to-Me ebook)
Subjects: LCSH: Othello (Shakespeare, William)--Juvenile fiction. | Othello (Fictitious character from Shakespeare)--Juvenile fiction. | Tragedy--Juvenile fiction. | Jealousy--Juvenile fiction. | Marriage--Juvenile fiction. | Literature--Juvenile fiction.
Classification: DDC 741.5--dc23

Table of Contents

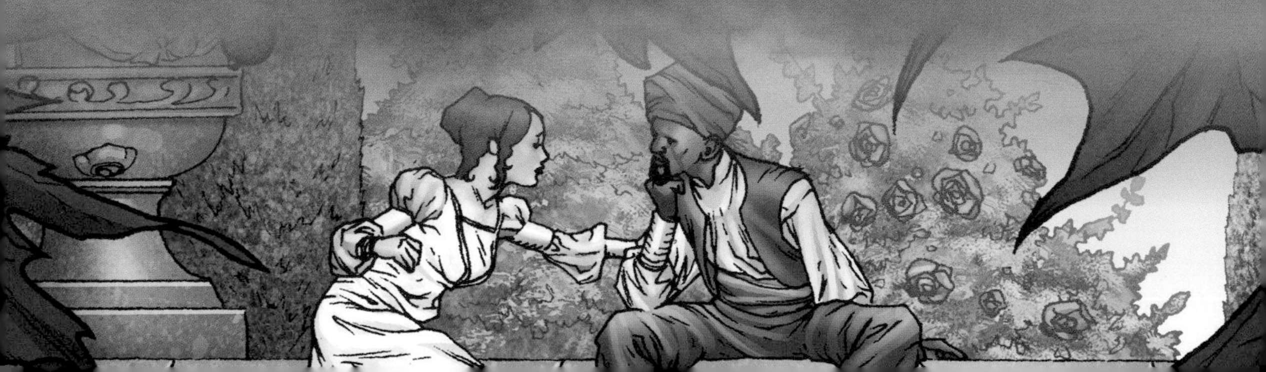

Cast of Characters

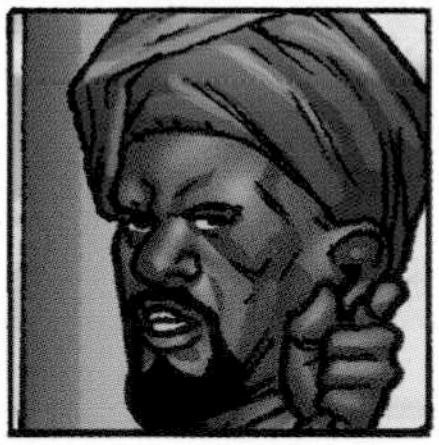

OTHELLO
The Moor

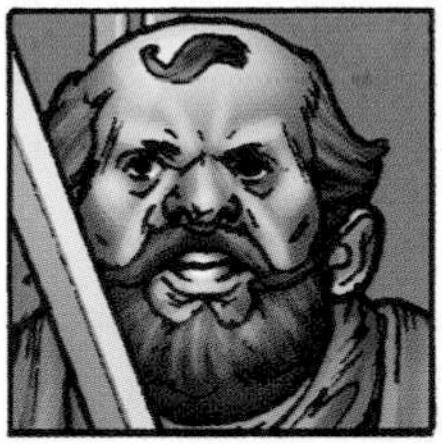

BRABANTIO
Father to Desdemona

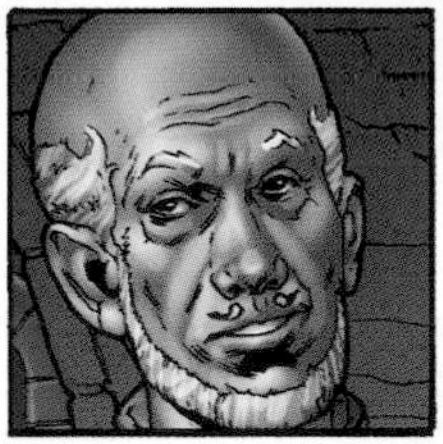

CASSIO
An honorable lieutenant

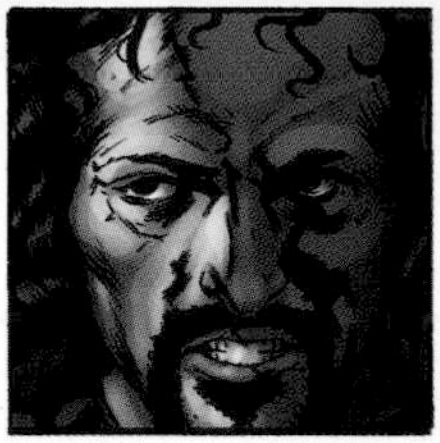

IAGO
A villain

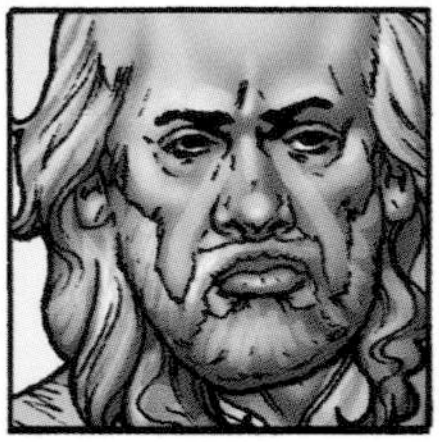

RODERIGO
A gentleman

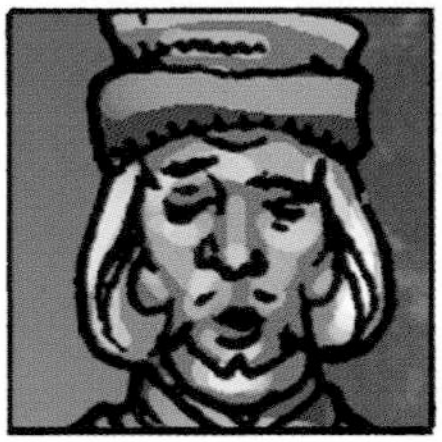

DUKE OF VENICE

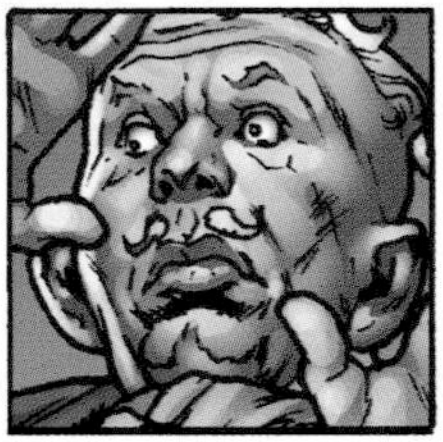

MONTANO
Governor of Cyprus

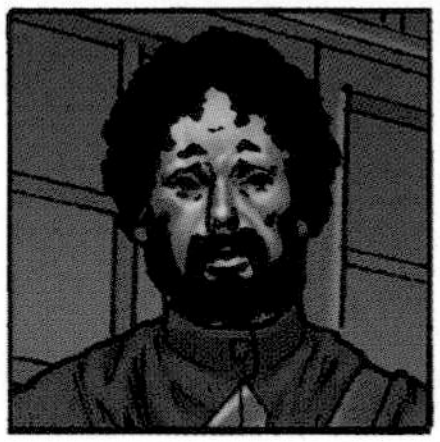

LODOVICO
Noble Venetian

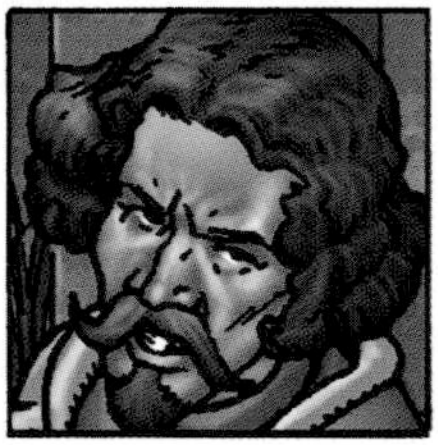

GATIANO
Noble Venetian

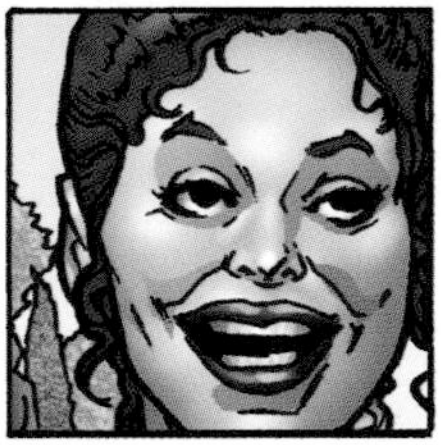

DESDEMONA
Wife to Othello

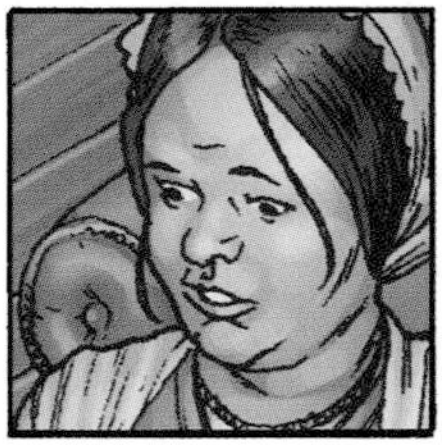

EMILIA
Wife to Iago

Synopsis

Iago is upset that his commander Othello has passed him over and has promoted Cassio. He complains about this to Roderigo and vows to get revenge. Iago asks Roderigo to tell Brabantio that his daughter Desdemona has married Othello. Brabantio opposes this because Othello is a Moor. Brabantio confronts Othello, and they present their grievance to the duke.

The duke has sent Othello to Cyprus to stop a Turkish invasion. Othello and Desdemona tell the duke they are in love. The duke gives Desdemona permission to travel to Cyprus with Othello. By the time they arrive, the Turkish threat is gone.

Iago and Roderigo manipulate Cassio into drinking too much and getting into a street fight. Othello demotes Cassio for his actions, and Iago has his revenge. To get back at Othello, Iago decides to get him to believe that Desdemona is unfaithful. He encourages Cassio to ask Desdemona for help to restore Cassio's position. Iago then suggests to Othello that Desdemona and Cassio might be lovers. Filled with jealousy, Othello promotes Iago and asks him to help kill Cassio and Desdemona.

Cassio asks Desdemona to intervene on his behalf with Othello and she agrees to help him. Meanwhile, Othello's jealousy has grown. He becomes upset when Desdemona cannot find a handkerchief Othello had given her, not knowing that Iago had instructed his wife, Emilia, to steal it. When Desdemona asks Othello to reconsider Cassio's loss of position, his jealousy intensifies. Iago leaves the handkerchief where Cassio will find it. Othello thinks Cassio's possession of the handkerchief is proof of Desdemona's unfaithfulness and moves forward with his evil plan.

Iago convinces Roderigo to kill Cassio. In the attack, Cassio wounds Roderigo, who is later killed by Iago. When Othello confronts Desdemona, she says she loves him. He smothers her, and as she dies she proclaims her innocence. Emilia recognizes Iago is behind everything. When Othello sees the truth he tries to kill Iago. Iago kills his wife and flees, but is captured later. Othello commits suicide and Iago is sentenced to death.

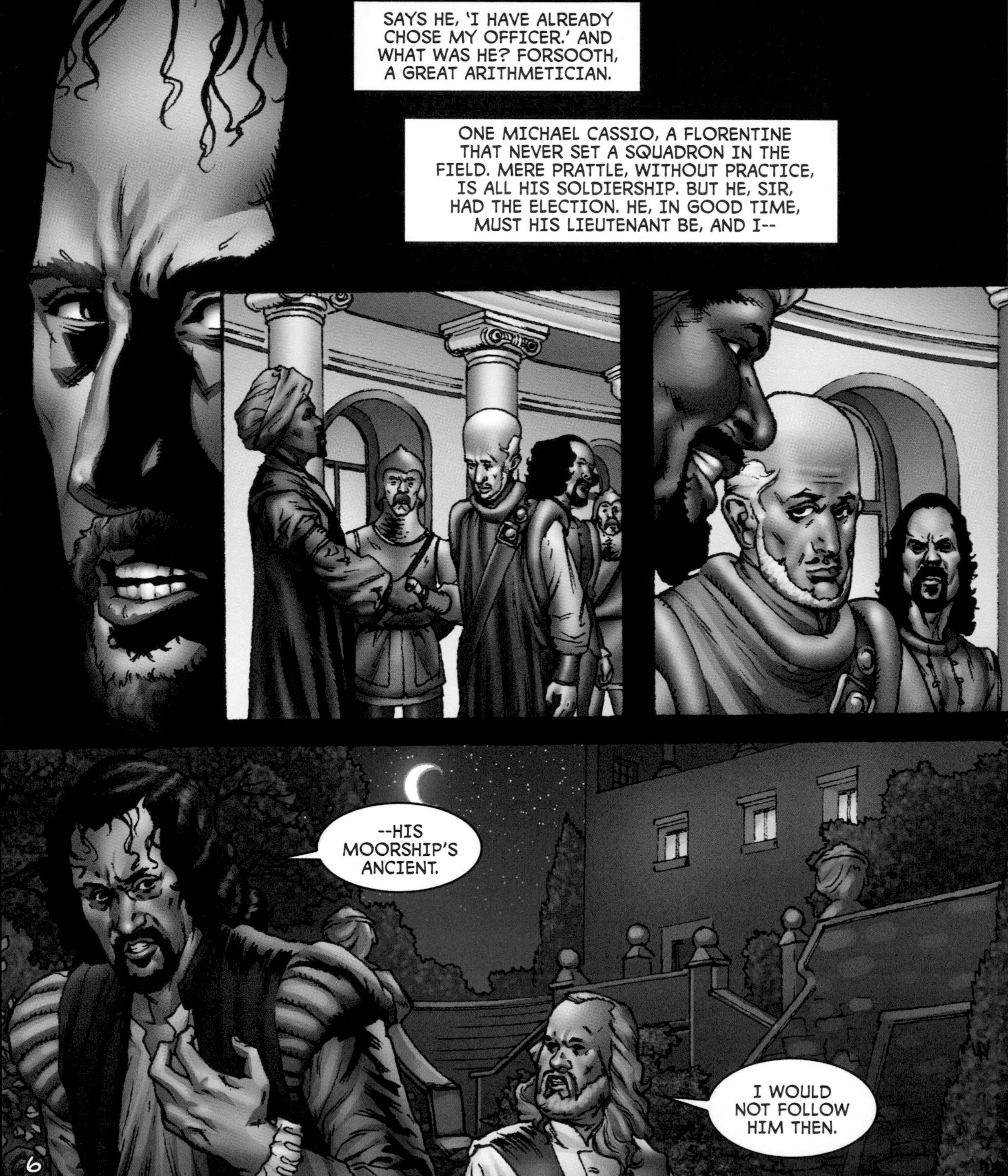
SAYS HE, 'I HAVE ALREADY CHOSE MY OFFICER.' AND WHAT WAS HE? FORSOOTH, A GREAT ARITHMETICIAN.
ONE MICHAEL CASSIO, A FLORENTINE THAT NEVER SET A SQUADRON IN THE FIELD. MERE PRATTLE, WITHOUT PRACTICE, IS ALL HIS SOLDIERSHIP. BUT HE, SIR, HAD THE ELECTION. HE, IN GOOD TIME, MUST HIS LIEUTENANT BE, AND I--
--HIS MOORSHIP'S ANCIENT.
I WOULD NOT FOLLOW HIM THEN.

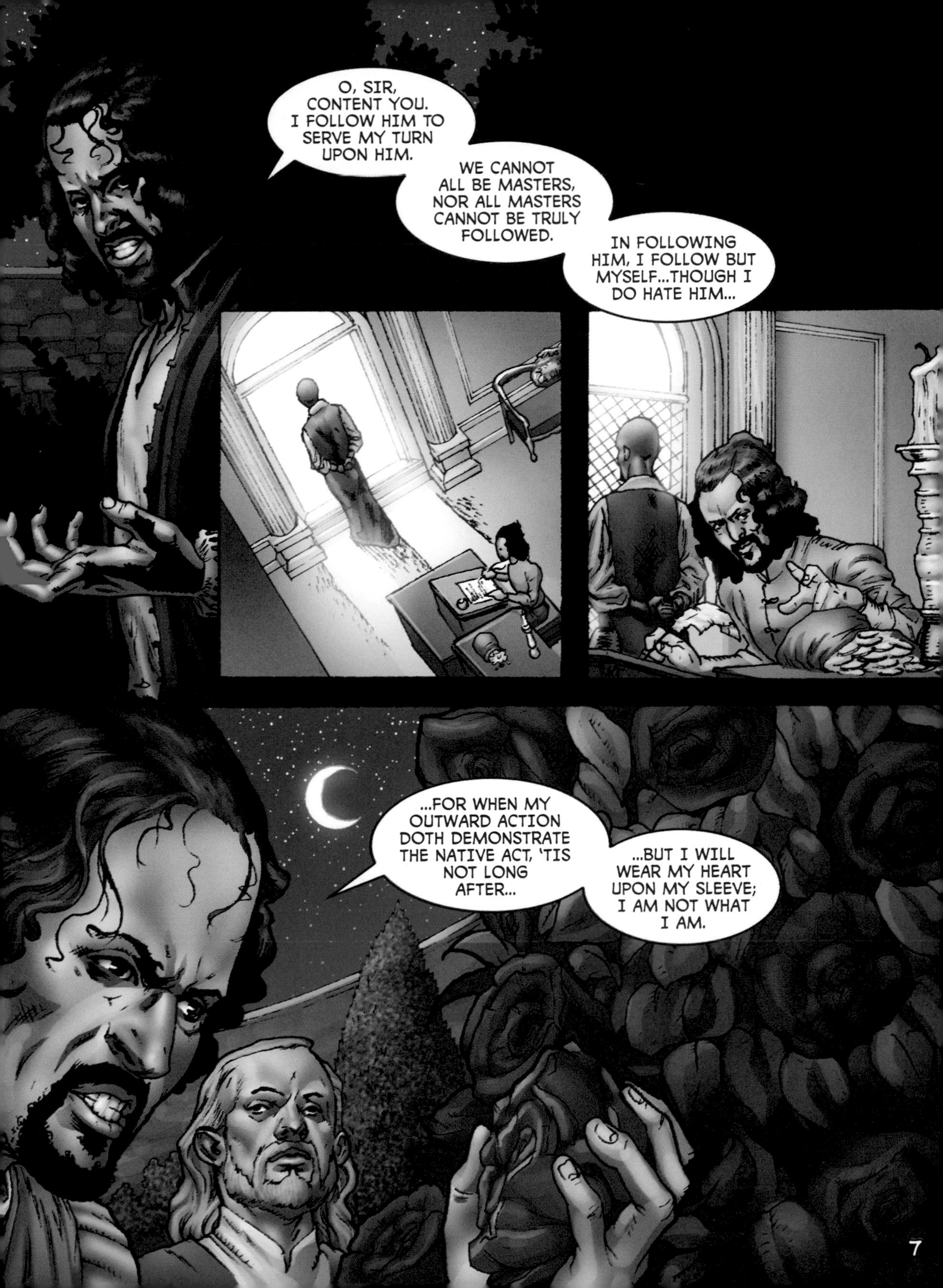
O, SIR, CONTENT YOU. I FOLLOW HIM TO SERVE MY TURN UPON HIM.
WE CANNOT ALL BE MASTERS, NOR ALL MASTERS CANNOT BE TRULY FOLLOWED.
IN FOLLOWING HIM, I FOLLOW BUT MYSELF...THOUGH I DO HATE HIM...
...FOR WHEN MY OUTWARD ACTION DOTH DEMONSTRATE THE NATIVE ACT, 'TIS NOT LONG AFTER...
...BUT I WILL WEAR MY HEART UPON MY SLEEVE; I AM NOT WHAT I AM.

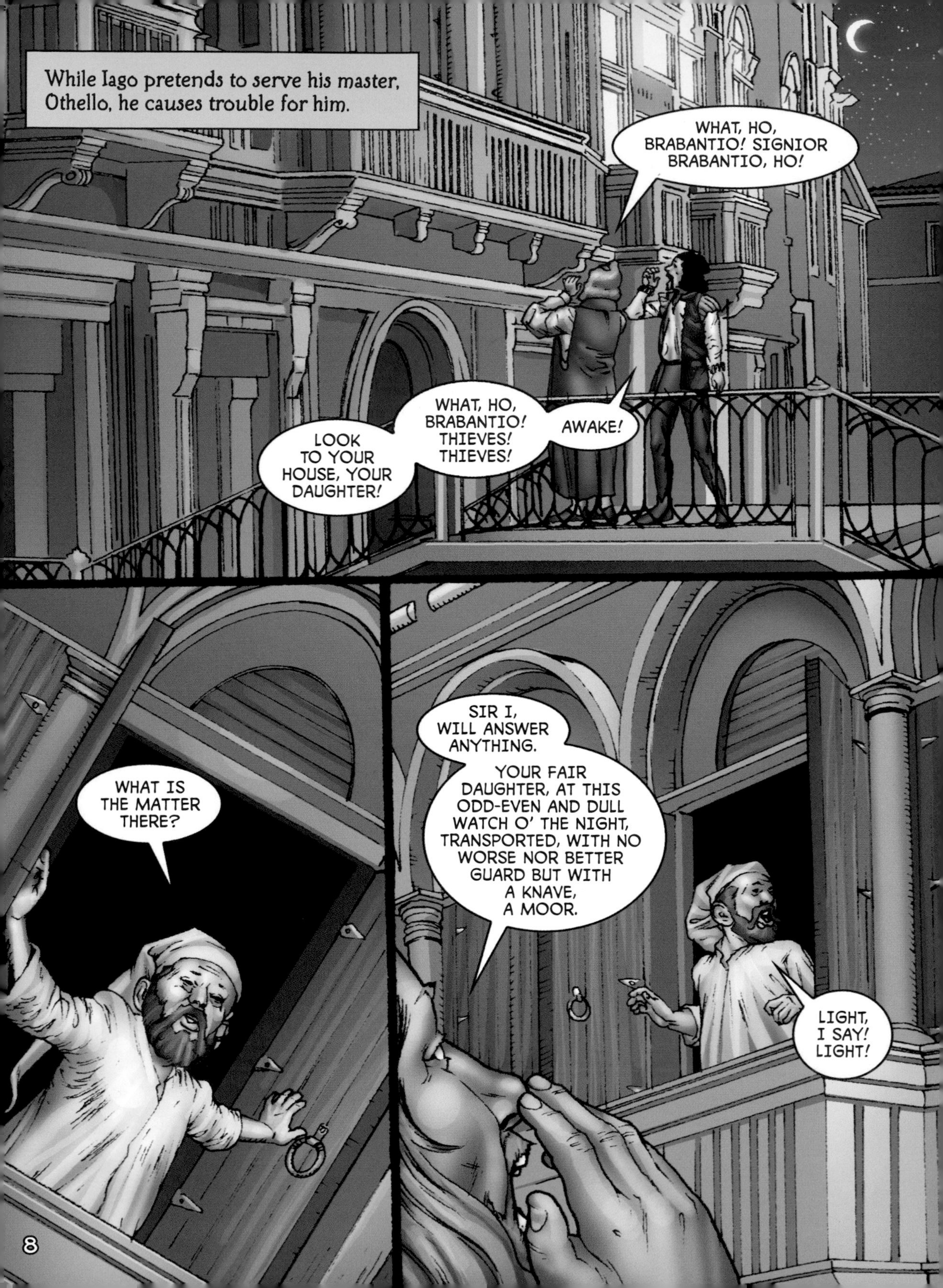
While Iago pretends to serve his master, Othello, he causes trouble for him.
WHAT, HO, BRABANTIO! SIGNIOR BRABANTIO, HO!
AWAKE!
WHAT, HO, BRABANTIO! THIEVES! THIEVES!
LOOK TO YOUR HOUSE, YOUR DAUGHTER!
WHAT IS THE MATTER THERE?
SIR I, WILL ANSWER ANYTHING.
YOUR FAIR DAUGHTER, AT THIS ODD-EVEN AND DULL WATCH O' THE NIGHT, TRANSPORTED, WITH NO WORSE NOR BETTER GUARD BUT WITH A KNAVE, A MOOR.
LIGHT, I SAY! LIGHT!

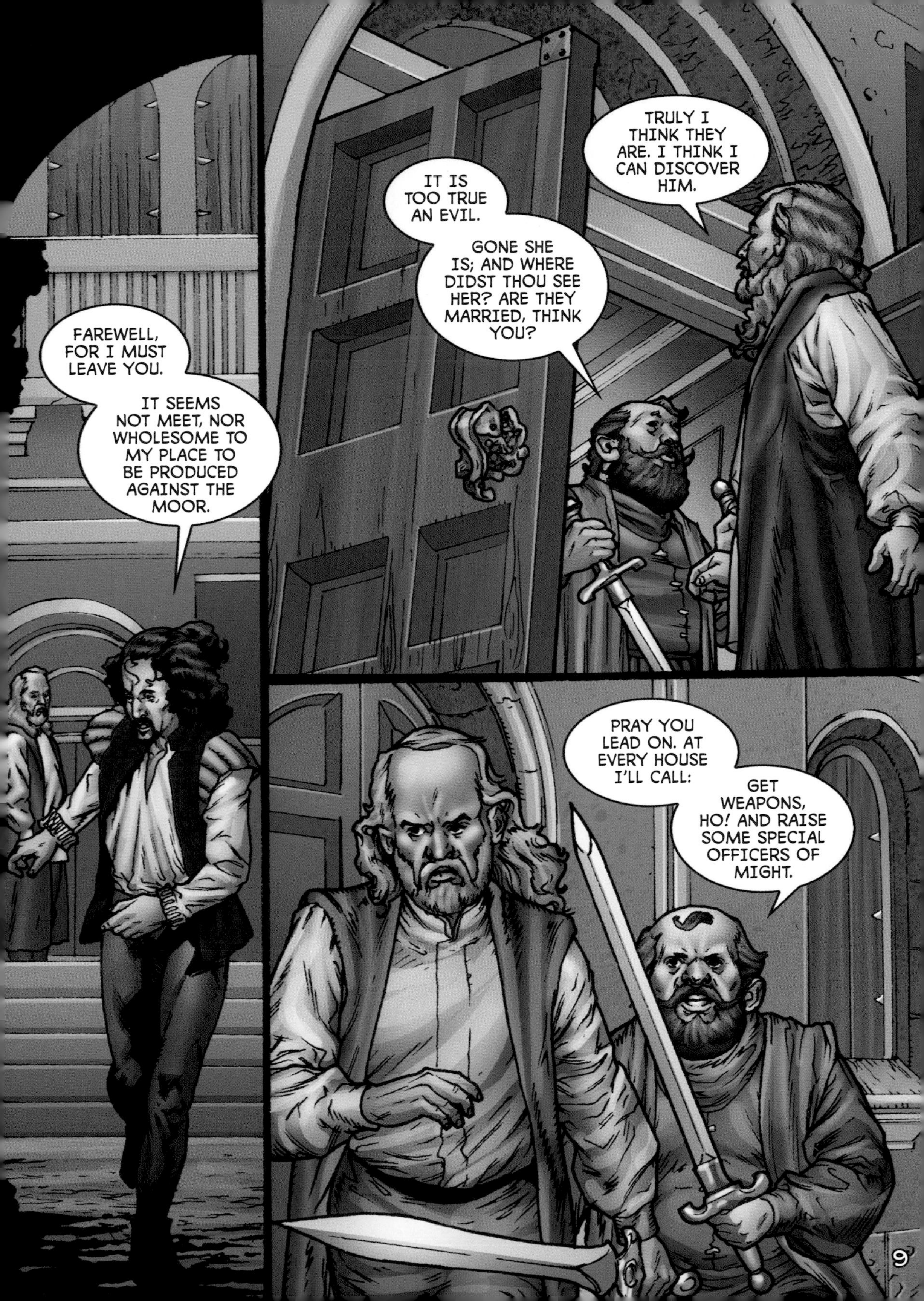
FAREWELL, FOR I MUST LEAVE YOU.
IT SEEMS NOT MEET, NOR WHOLESOME TO MY PLACE TO BE PRODUCED AGAINST THE MOOR.
IT IS TOO TRUE AN EVIL.
GONE SHE IS; AND WHERE DIDST THOU SEE HER? ARE THEY MARRIED, THINK YOU?
TRULY I THINK THEY ARE. I THINK I CAN DISCOVER HIM.
PRAY YOU LEAD ON. AT EVERY HOUSE I'LL CALL:
GET WEAPONS, HO! AND RAISE SOME SPECIAL OFFICERS OF MIGHT.

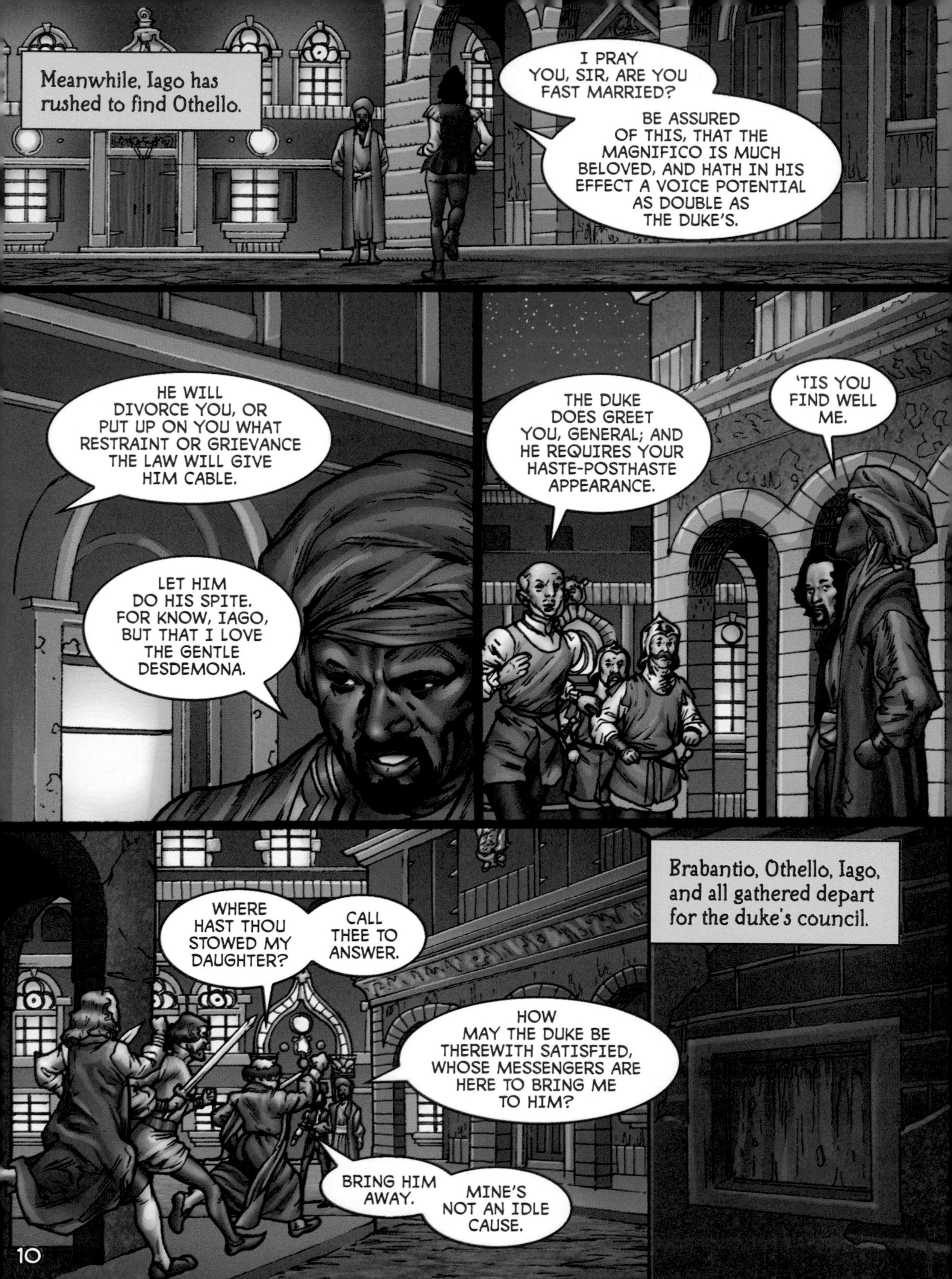
Meanwhile, Iago has rushed to find Othello.
I PRAY YOU, SIR, ARE YOU FAST MARRIED?
BE ASSURED OF THIS, THAT THE MAGNIFICO IS MUCH BELOVED, AND HATH IN HIS EFFECT A VOICE POTENTIAL AS DOUBLE AS THE DUKE'S.
HE WILL DIVORCE YOU, OR PUT UP ON YOU WHAT RESTRAINT OR GRIEVANCE THE LAW WILL GIVE HIM CABLE.
LET HIM DO HIS SPITE. FOR KNOW, IAGO, BUT THAT I LOVE THE GENTLE DESDEMONA.
THE DUKE DOES GREET YOU, GENERAL; AND HE REQUIRES YOUR HASTE-POSTHASTE APPEARANCE.
'TIS YOU FIND WELL ME.
Brabantio, Othello, Iago, and all gathered depart for the duke's council.
WHERE HAST THOU STOWED MY DAUGHTER?
CALL THEE TO ANSWER.
HOW MAY THE DUKE BE THEREWITH SATISFIED, WHOSE MESSENGERS ARE HERE TO BRING ME TO HIM?
BRING HIM AWAY.
MINE'S NOT AN IDLE CAUSE.

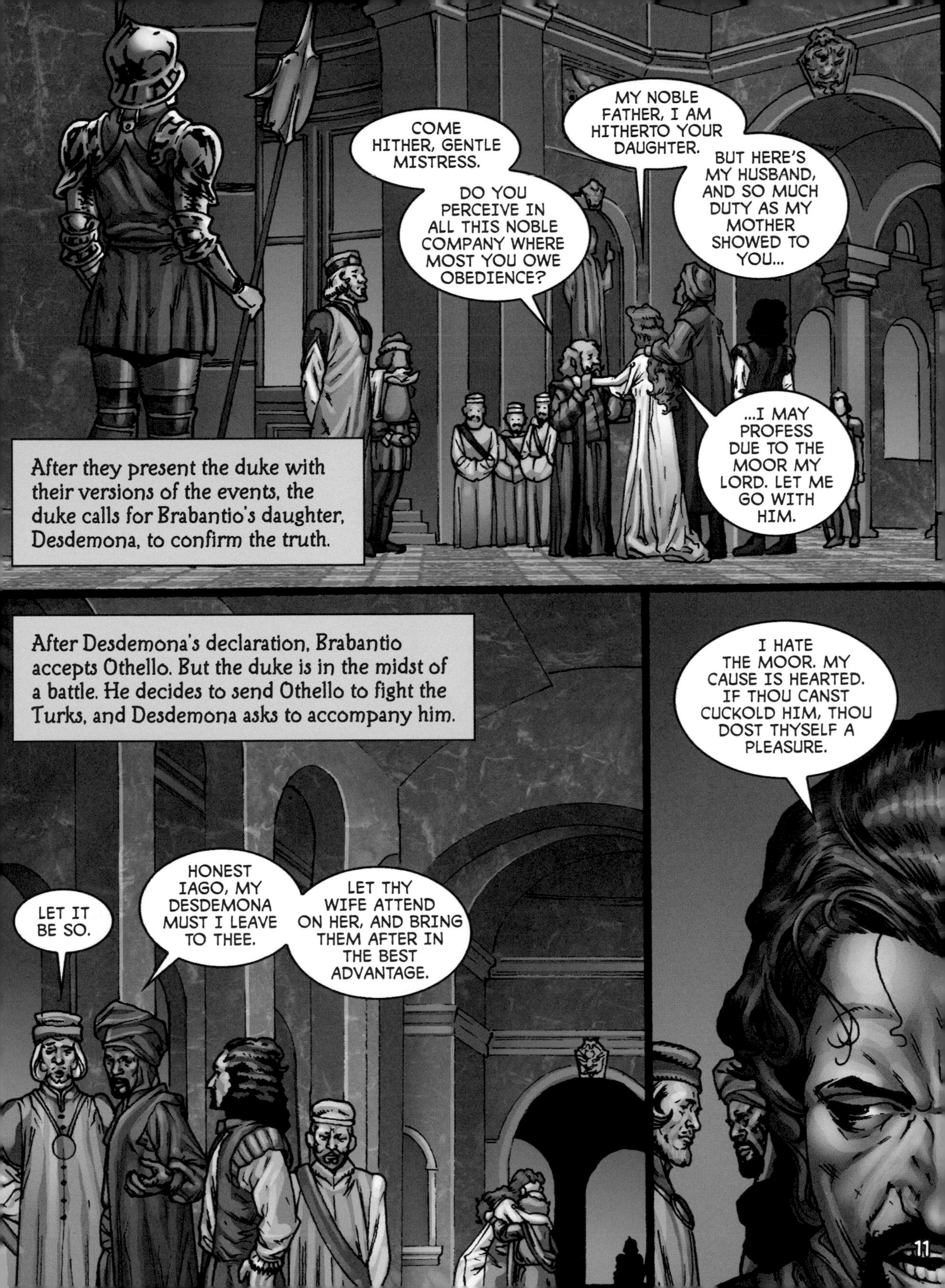
After they present the duke with their versions of the events, the duke calls for Brabantio's daughter, Desdemona, to confirm the truth.
COME HITHER, GENTLE MISTRESS.
DO YOU PERCEIVE IN ALL THIS NOBLE COMPANY WHERE MOST YOU OWE OBEDIENCE?
MY NOBLE FATHER, I AM HITHERTO YOUR DAUGHTER.
BUT HERE'S MY HUSBAND, AND SO MUCH DUTY AS MY MOTHER SHOWED TO YOU...
...I MAY PROFESS DUE TO THE MOOR MY LORD. LET ME GO WITH HIM.
After Desdemona's declaration, Brabantio accepts Othello. But the duke is in the midst of a battle. He decides to send Othello to fight the Turks, and Desdemona asks to accompany him.
LET IT BE SO.
HONEST IAGO, MY DESDEMONA MUST I LEAVE TO THEE.
LET THY WIFE ATTEND ON HER, AND BRING THEM AFTER IN THE BEST ADVANTAGE.
I HATE THE MOOR. MY CAUSE IS HEARTED. IF THOU CANST CUCKOLD HIM, THOU DOST THYSELF A PLEASURE.

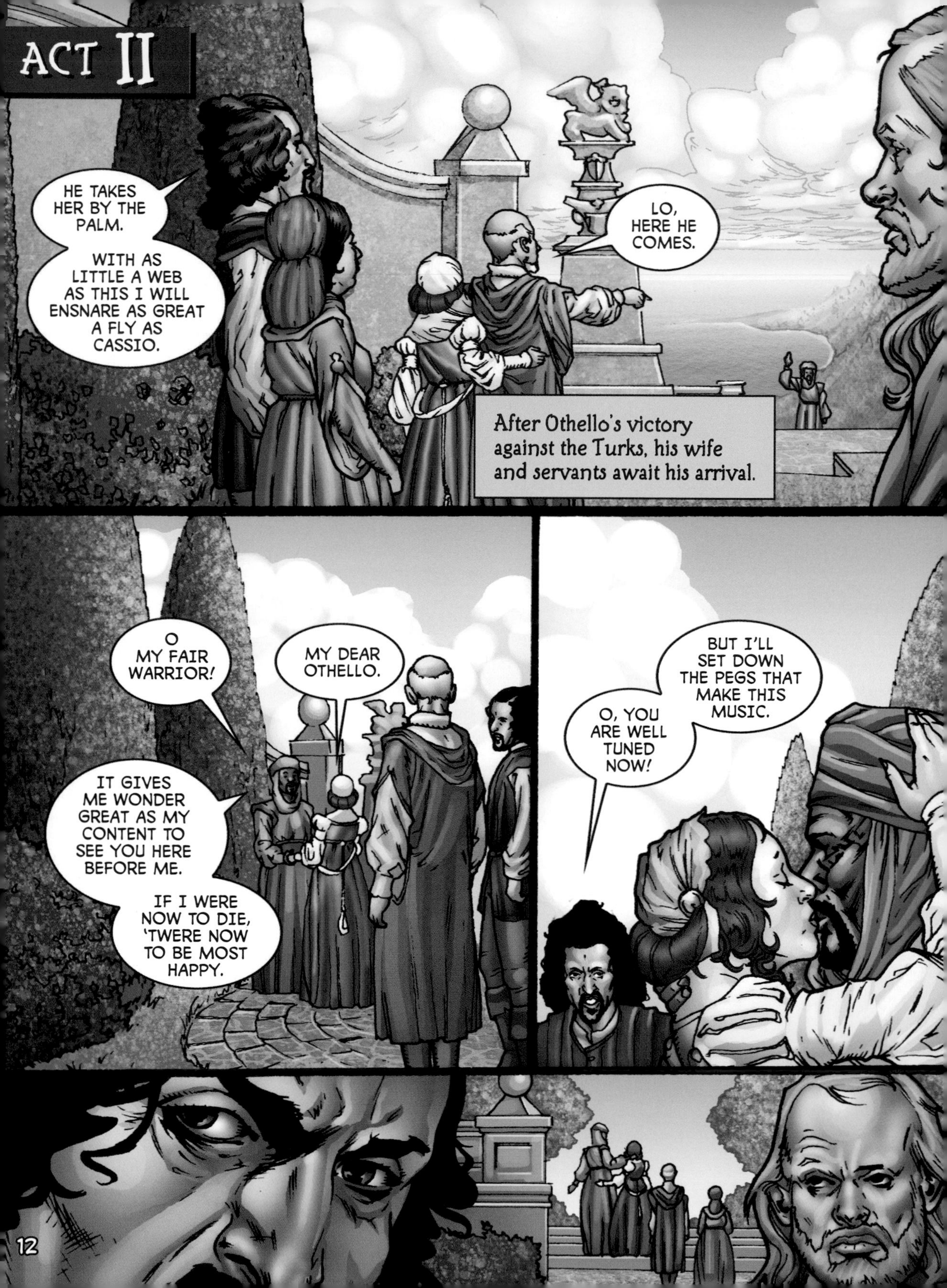
ACT II
HE TAKES HER BY THE PALM.
WITH AS LITTLE A WEB AS THIS I WILL ENSNARE AS GREAT A FLY AS CASSIO.
LO, HERE HE COMES.
After Othello's victory against the Turks, his wife and servants await his arrival.
O MY FAIR WARRIOR!
MY DEAR OTHELLO.
IT GIVES ME WONDER GREAT AS MY CONTENT TO SEE YOU HERE BEFORE ME.
IF I WERE NOW TO DIE, 'TWERE NOW TO BE MOST HAPPY.
O, YOU ARE WELL TUNED NOW!
BUT I'LL SET DOWN THE PEGS THAT MAKE THIS MUSIC.

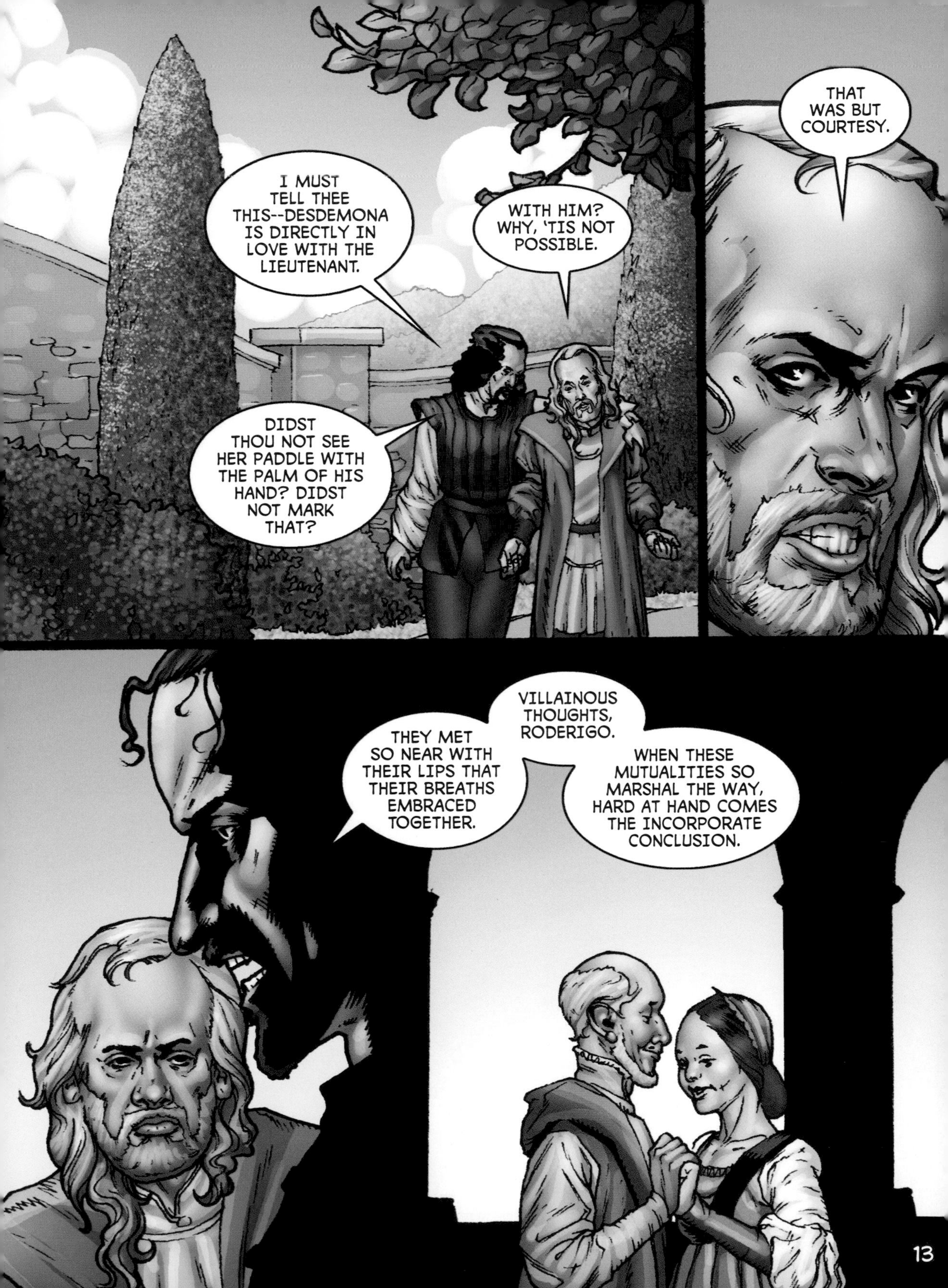
I MUST TELL THEE THIS--DESDEMONA IS DIRECTLY IN LOVE WITH THE LIEUTENANT.
WITH HIM? WHY, 'TIS NOT POSSIBLE.
DIDST THOU NOT SEE HER PADDLE WITH THE PALM OF HIS HAND? DIDST NOT MARK THAT?
THAT WAS BUT COURTESY.
THEY MET SO NEAR WITH THEIR LIPS THAT THEIR BREATHS EMBRACED TOGETHER.
VILLAINOUS THOUGHTS, RODERIGO.
WHEN THESE MUTUALITIES SO MARSHAL THE WAY, HARD AT HAND COMES THE INCORPORATE CONCLUSION.

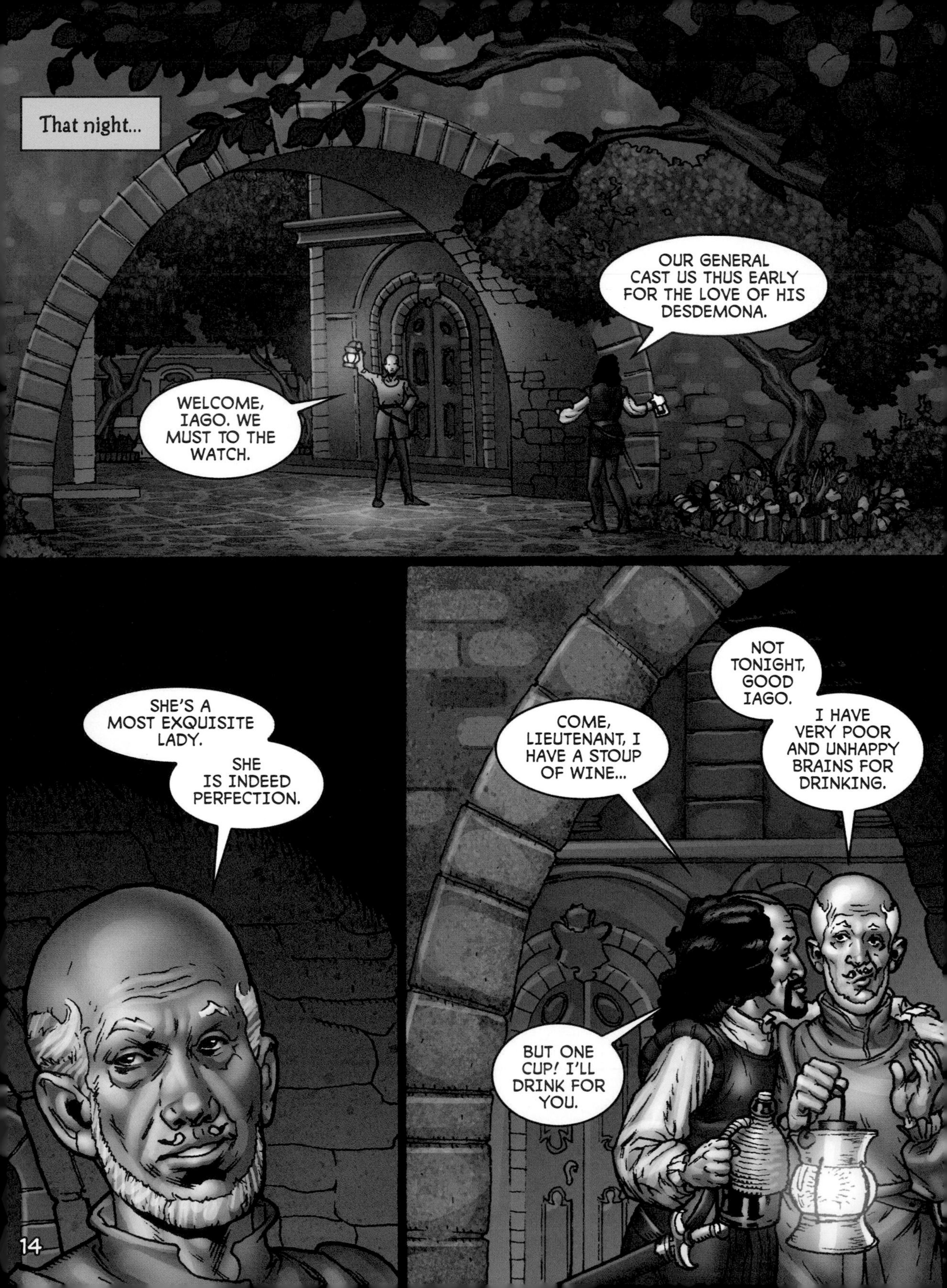
That night...
WELCOME, IAGO. WE MUST TO THE WATCH.
OUR GENERAL CAST US THUS EARLY FOR THE LOVE OF HIS DESDEMONA.
SHE'S A MOST EXQUISITE LADY.
SHE IS INDEED PERFECTION.
COME, LIEUTENANT, I HAVE A STOUP OF WINE...
NOT TONIGHT, GOOD IAGO.
I HAVE VERY POOR AND UNHAPPY BRAINS FOR DRINKING.
BUT ONE CUP! I'LL DRINK FOR YOU.

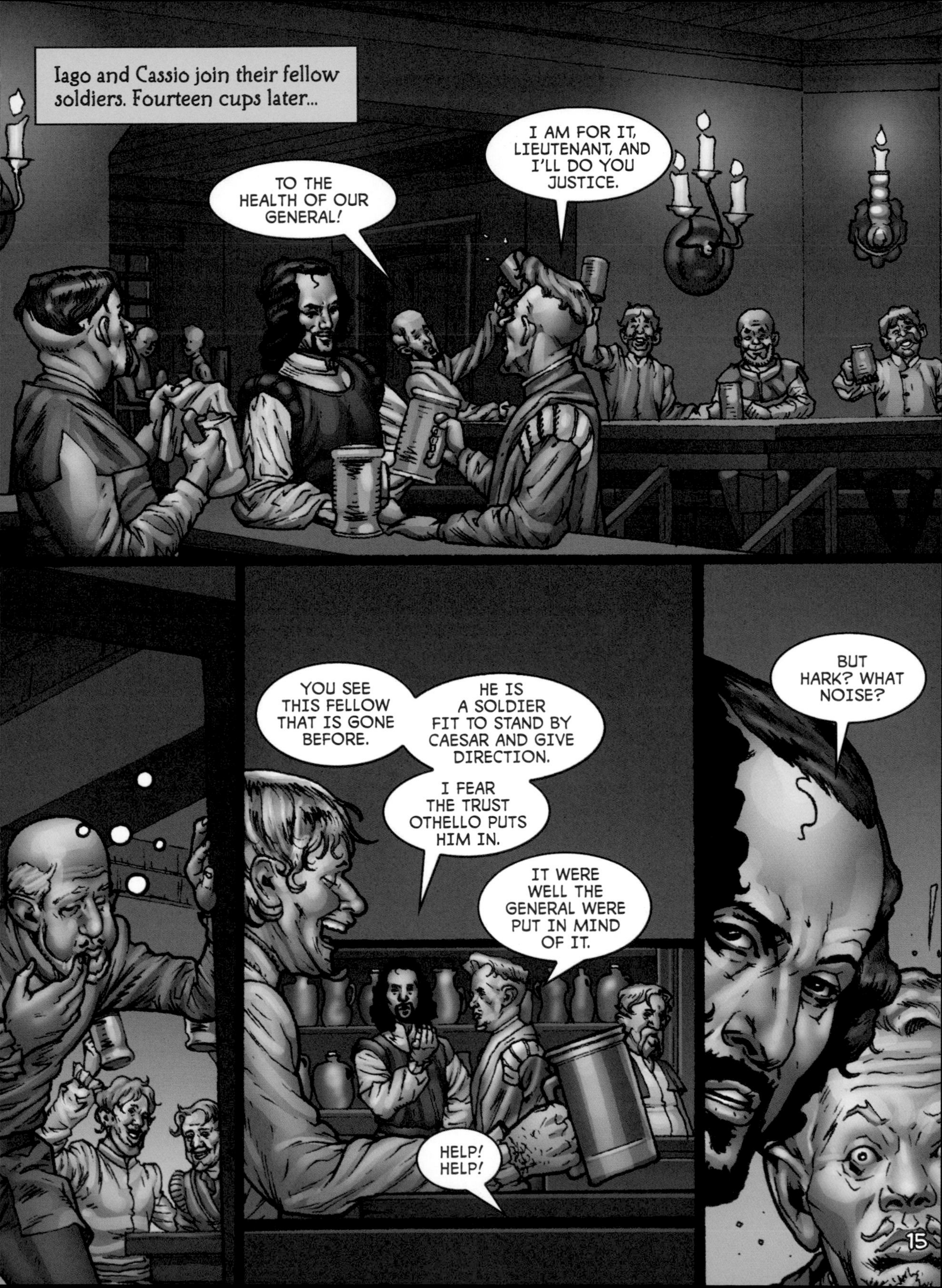

Iago and Cassio join their fellow soldiers. Fourteen cups later...
TO THE HEALTH OF OUR GENERAL!
I AM FOR IT, LIEUTENANT, AND I'LL DO YOU JUSTICE.
YOU SEE THIS FELLOW THAT IS GONE BEFORE.
HE IS A SOLDIER FIT TO STAND BY CAESAR AND GIVE DIRECTION.
I FEAR THE TRUST OTHELLO PUTS HIM IN.
IT WERE WELL THE GENERAL WERE PUT IN MIND OF IT.
HELP! HELP!
BUT HARK? WHAT NOISE?

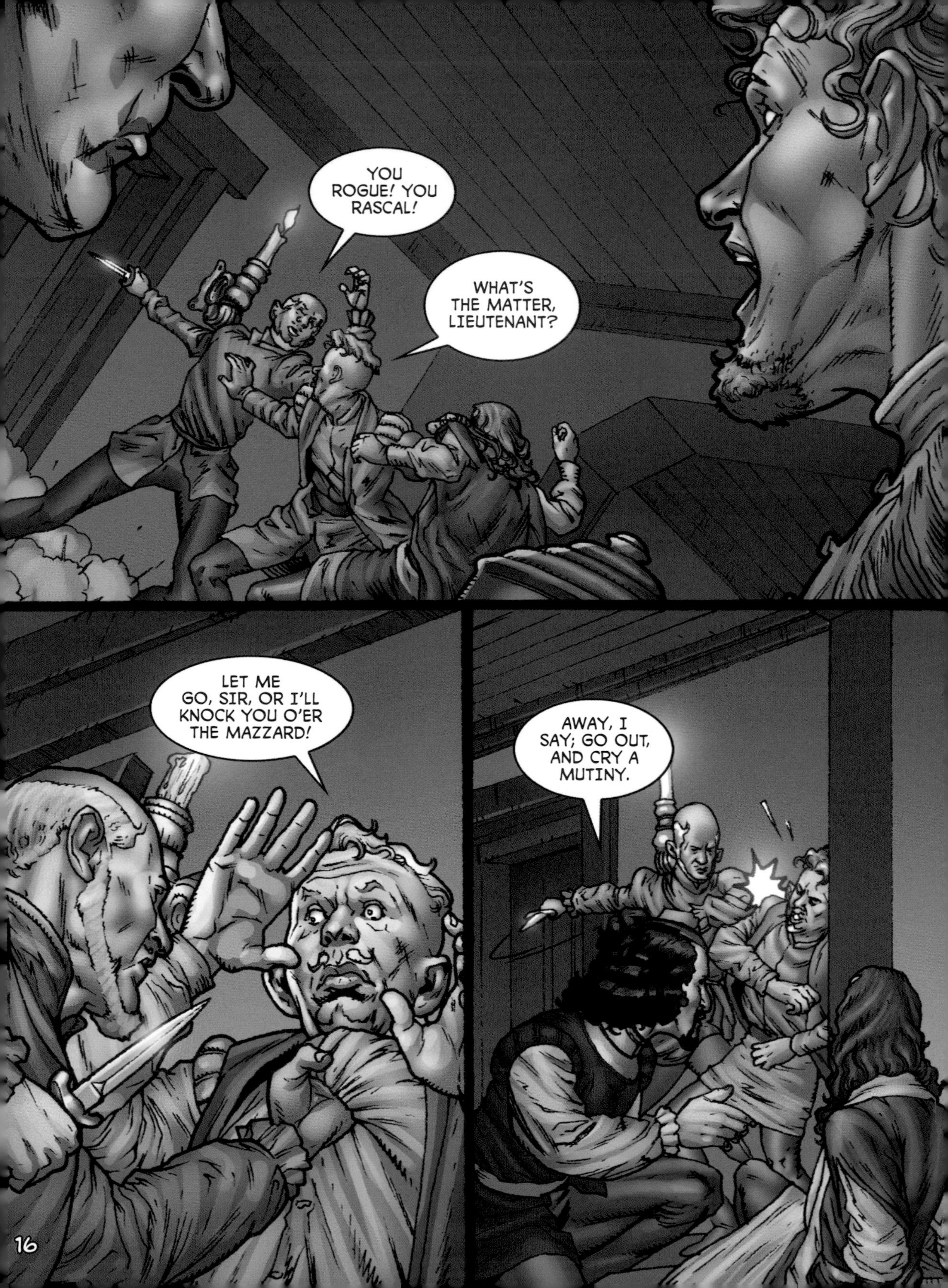
YOU ROGUE! YOU RASCAL!
WHAT'S THE MATTER, LIEUTENANT?
LET ME GO, SIR, OR I'LL KNOCK YOU O'ER THE MAZZARD!
AWAY, I SAY; GO OUT, AND CRY A MUTINY.

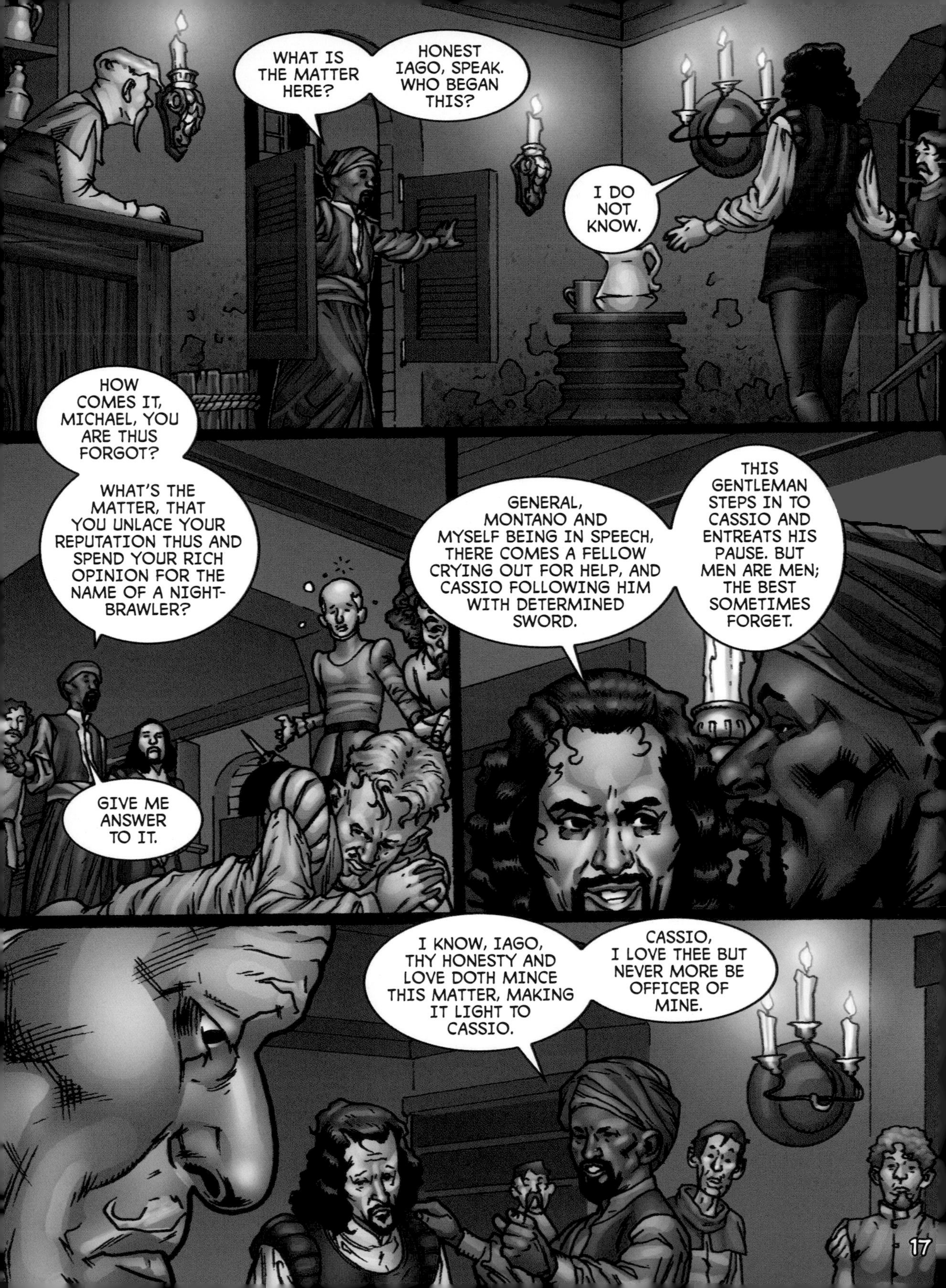
WHAT IS THE MATTER HERE?
HONEST IAGO, SPEAK. WHO BEGAN THIS?
I DO NOT KNOW.
HOW COMES IT, MICHAEL, YOU ARE THUS FORGOT?
WHAT'S THE MATTER, THAT YOU UNLACE YOUR REPUTATION THUS AND SPEND YOUR RICH OPINION FOR THE NAME OF A NIGHT-BRAWLER?
GIVE ME ANSWER TO IT.
GENERAL, MONTANO AND MYSELF BEING IN SPEECH, THERE COMES A FELLOW CRYING OUT FOR HELP, AND CASSIO FOLLOWING HIM WITH DETERMINED SWORD.
THIS GENTLEMAN STEPS IN TO CASSIO AND ENTREATS HIS PAUSE. BUT MEN ARE MEN; THE BEST SOMETIMES FORGET.
I KNOW, IAGO, THY HONESTY AND LOVE DOTH MINCE THIS MATTER, MAKING IT LIGHT TO CASSIO.
CASSIO, I LOVE THEE BUT NEVER MORE BE OFFICER OF MINE.

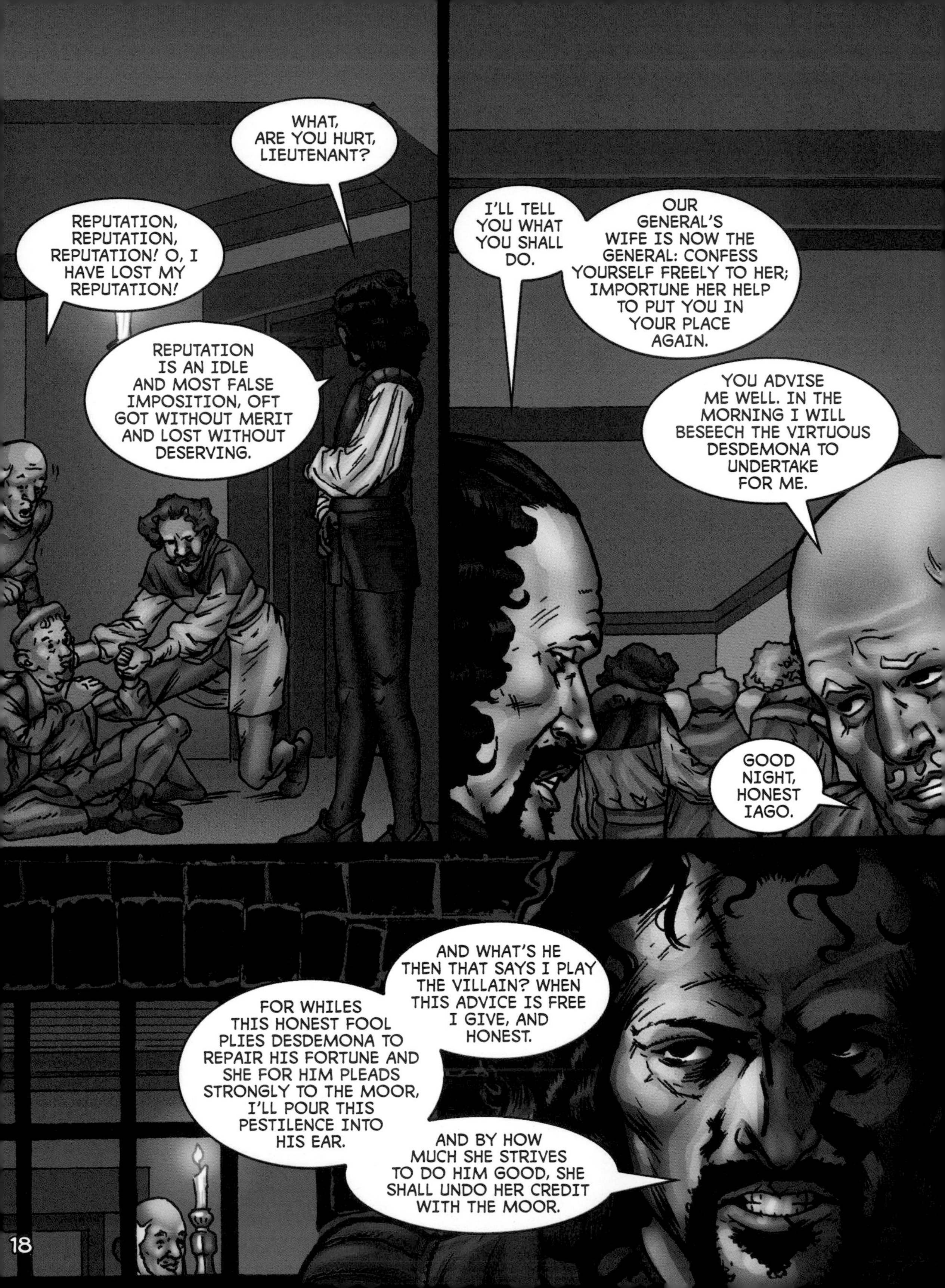
WHAT, ARE YOU HURT, LIEUTENANT?
REPUTATION, REPUTATION, REPUTATION! O, I HAVE LOST MY REPUTATION!
REPUTATION IS AN IDLE AND MOST FALSE IMPOSITION, OFT GOT WITHOUT MERIT AND LOST WITHOUT DESERVING.
I'LL TELL YOU WHAT YOU SHALL DO.
OUR GENERAL'S WIFE IS NOW THE GENERAL: CONFESS YOURSELF FREELY TO HER; IMPORTUNE HER HELP TO PUT YOU IN YOUR PLACE AGAIN.
YOU ADVISE ME WELL. IN THE MORNING I WILL BESEECH THE VIRTUOUS DESDEMONA TO UNDERTAKE FOR ME.
GOOD NIGHT, HONEST IAGO.
AND WHAT'S HE THEN THAT SAYS I PLAY THE VILLAIN? WHEN THIS ADVICE IS FREE I GIVE, AND HONEST.
FOR WHILES THIS HONEST FOOL PLIES DESDEMONA TO REPAIR HIS FORTUNE AND SHE FOR HIM PLEADS STRONGLY TO THE MOOR, I'LL POUR THIS PESTILENCE INTO HIS EAR.
AND BY HOW MUCH SHE STRIVES TO DO HIM GOOD, SHE SHALL UNDO HER CREDIT WITH THE MOOR.

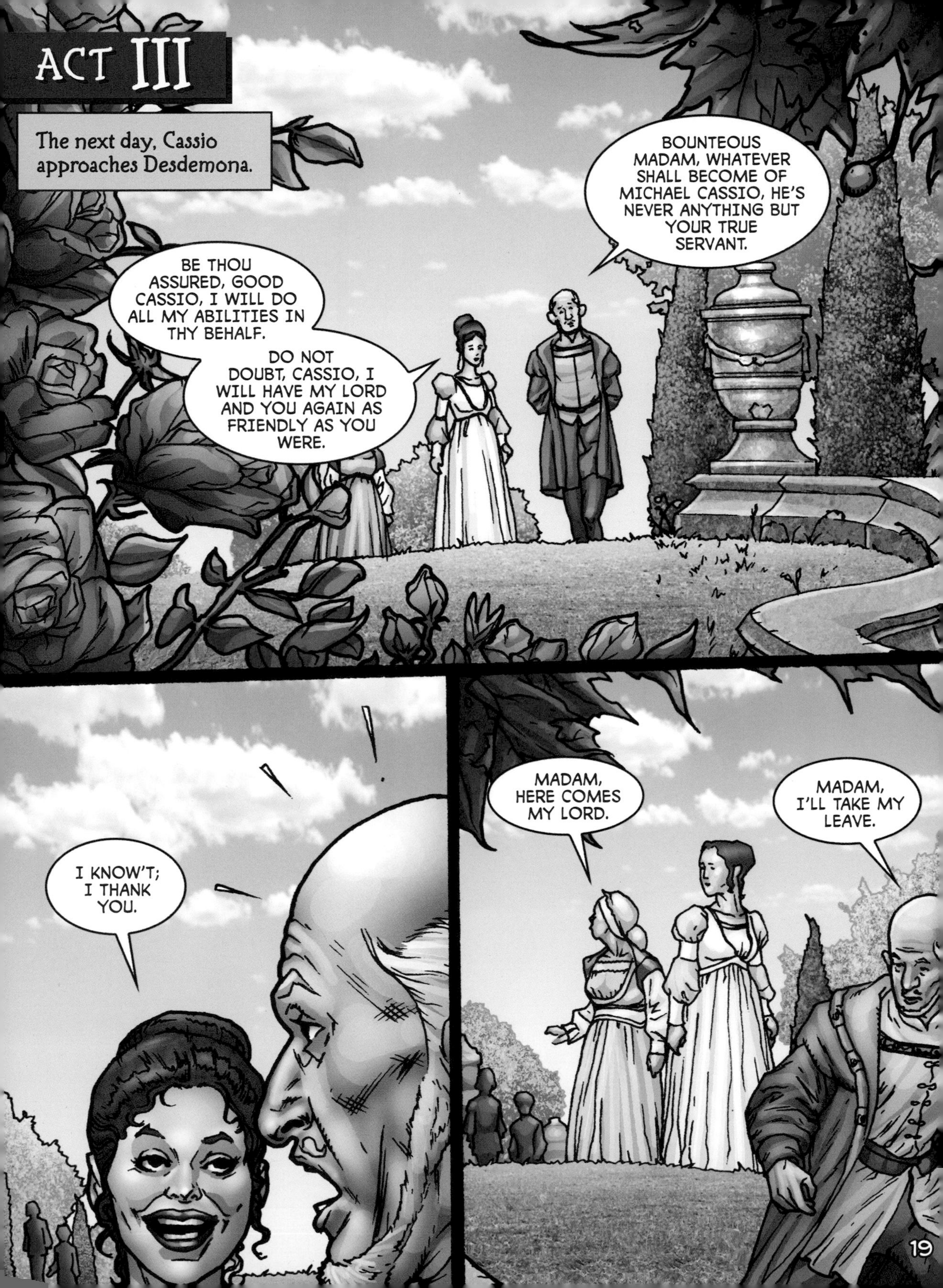
ACT III
The next day, Cassio approaches Desdemona.
BOUNTEOUS MADAM, WHATEVER SHALL BECOME OF MICHAEL CASSIO, HE'S NEVER ANYTHING BUT YOUR TRUE SERVANT.
BE THOU ASSURED, GOOD CASSIO, I WILL DO ALL MY ABILITIES IN THY BEHALF.
DO NOT DOUBT, CASSIO, I WILL HAVE MY LORD AND YOU AGAIN AS FRIENDLY AS YOU WERE.
I KNOW'T; I THANK YOU.
MADAM, HERE COMES MY LORD.
MADAM, I'LL TAKE MY LEAVE.

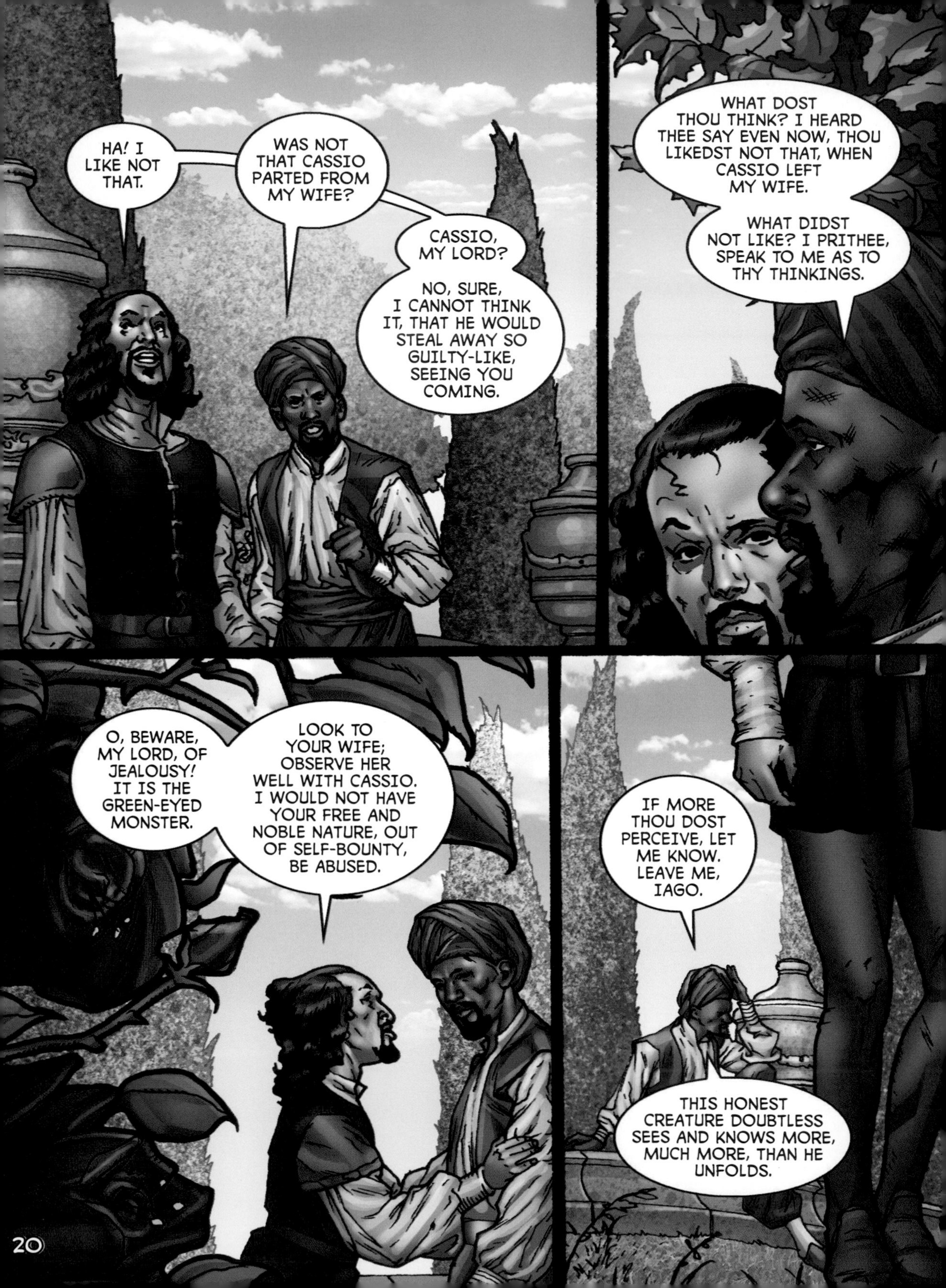
HA! I LIKE NOT THAT.
WAS NOT THAT CASSIO PARTED FROM MY WIFE?
CASSIO, MY LORD?
NO, SURE, I CANNOT THINK IT, THAT HE WOULD STEAL AWAY SO GUILTY-LIKE, SEEING YOU COMING.
WHAT DOST THOU THINK? I HEARD THEE SAY EVEN NOW, THOU LIKEDST NOT THAT, WHEN CASSIO LEFT MY WIFE.
WHAT DIDST NOT LIKE? I PRITHEE, SPEAK TO ME AS TO THY THINKINGS.
O, BEWARE, MY LORD, OF JEALOUSY! IT IS THE GREEN-EYED MONSTER.
LOOK TO YOUR WIFE; OBSERVE HER WELL WITH CASSIO. I WOULD NOT HAVE YOUR FREE AND NOBLE NATURE, OUT OF SELF-BOUNTY, BE ABUSED.
IF MORE THOU DOST PERCEIVE, LET ME KNOW. LEAVE ME, IAGO.
THIS HONEST CREATURE DOUBTLESS SEES AND KNOWS MORE, MUCH MORE, THAN HE UNFOLDS.

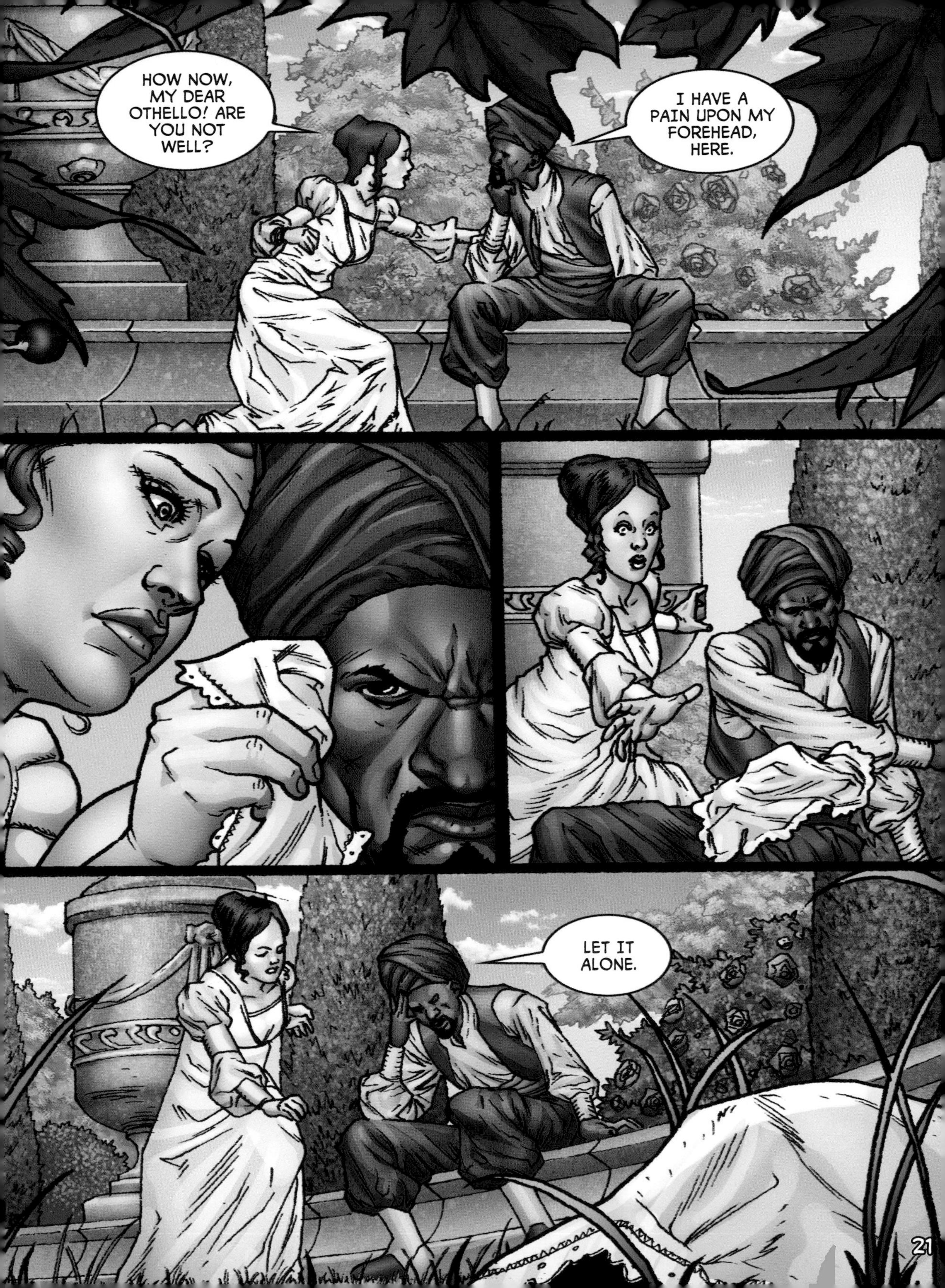
HOW NOW, MY DEAR OTHELLO! ARE YOU NOT WELL?
I HAVE A PAIN UPON MY FOREHEAD, HERE.
LET IT ALONE.

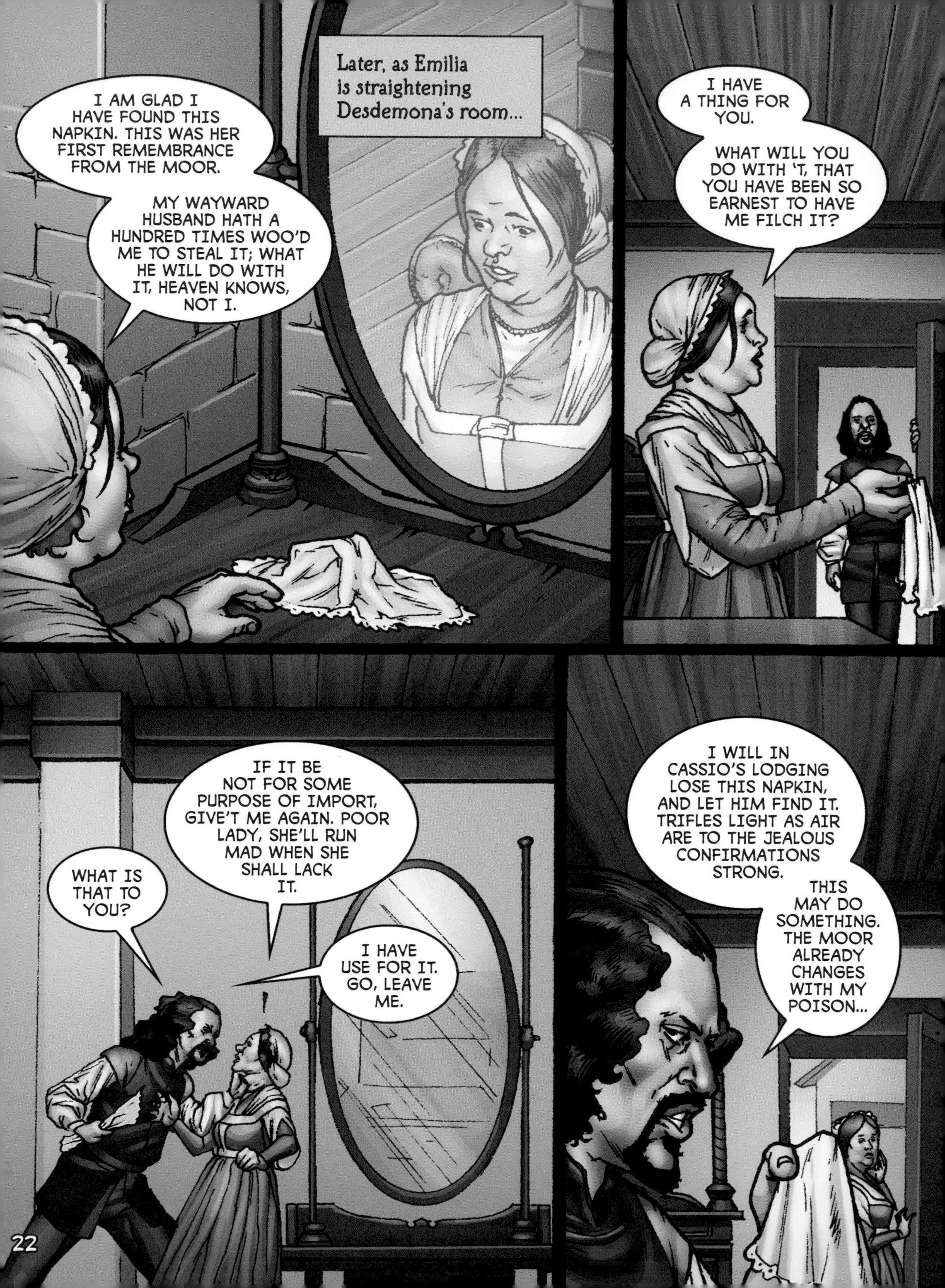
Later, as Emilia is straightening Desdemona's room...
I AM GLAD I HAVE FOUND THIS NAPKIN. THIS WAS HER FIRST REMEMBRANCE FROM THE MOOR.
MY WAYWARD HUSBAND HATH A HUNDRED TIMES WOO'D ME TO STEAL IT; WHAT HE WILL DO WITH IT, HEAVEN KNOWS, NOT I.
I HAVE A THING FOR YOU.
WHAT WILL YOU DO WITH 'T, THAT YOU HAVE BEEN SO EARNEST TO HAVE ME FILCH IT?
WHAT IS THAT TO YOU?
IF IT BE NOT FOR SOME PURPOSE OF IMPORT, GIVE'T ME AGAIN. POOR LADY, SHE'LL RUN MAD WHEN SHE SHALL LACK IT.
I HAVE USE FOR IT. GO, LEAVE ME.
I WILL IN CASSIO'S LODGING LOSE THIS NAPKIN, AND LET HIM FIND IT. TRIFLES LIGHT AS AIR ARE TO THE JEALOUS CONFIRMATIONS STRONG.
THIS MAY DO SOMETHING. THE MOOR ALREADY CHANGES WITH MY POISON...

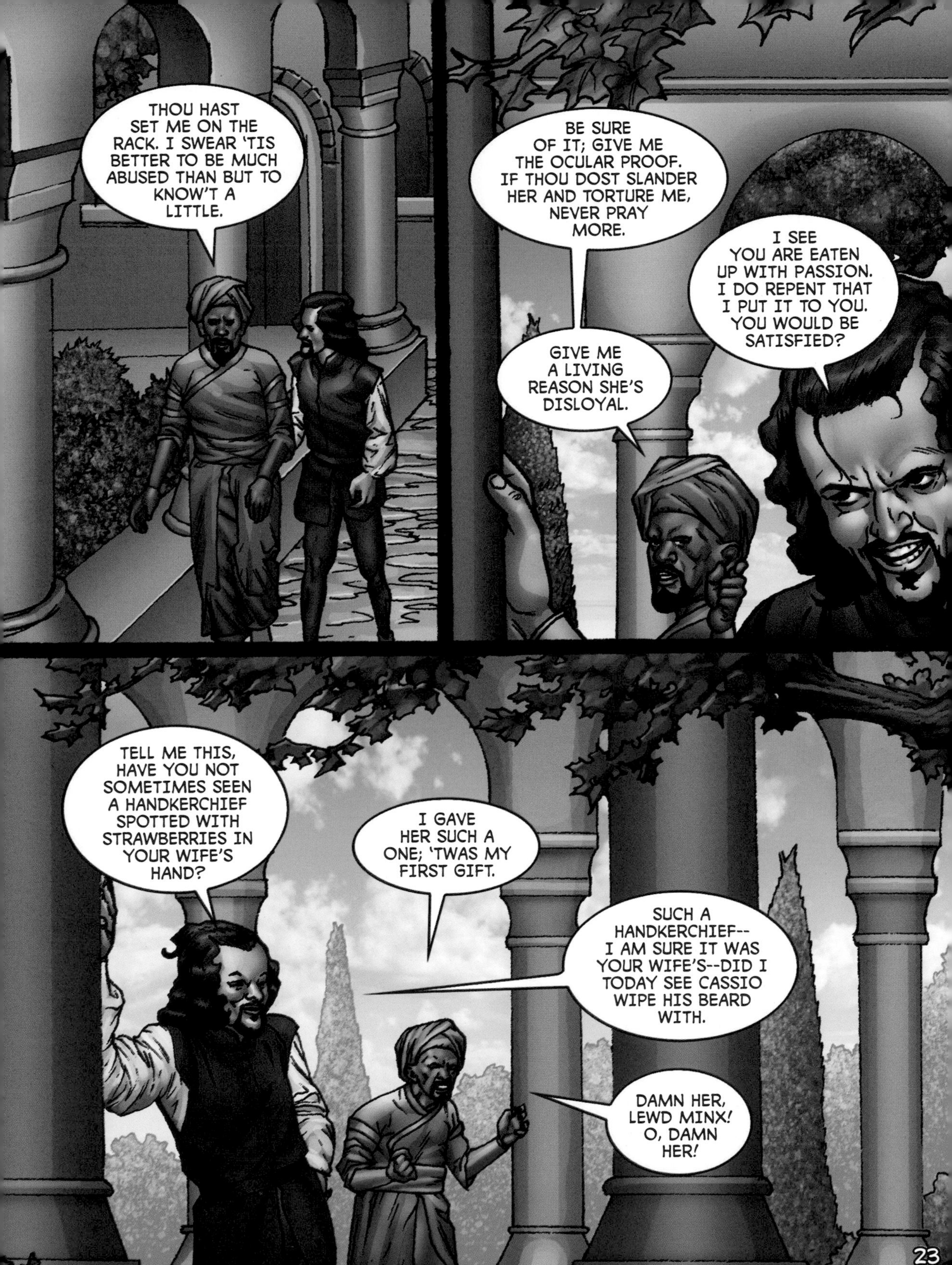
THOU HAST SET ME ON THE RACK. I SWEAR 'TIS BETTER TO BE MUCH ABUSED THAN BUT TO KNOW'T A LITTLE.
BE SURE OF IT; GIVE ME THE OCULAR PROOF. IF THOU DOST SLANDER HER AND TORTURE ME, NEVER PRAY MORE.
I SEE YOU ARE EATEN UP WITH PASSION. I DO REPENT THAT I PUT IT TO YOU. YOU WOULD BE SATISFIED?
GIVE ME A LIVING REASON SHE'S DISLOYAL.
TELL ME THIS, HAVE YOU NOT SOMETIMES SEEN A HANDKERCHIEF SPOTTED WITH STRAWBERRIES IN YOUR WIFE'S HAND?
I GAVE HER SUCH A ONE; 'TWAS MY FIRST GIFT.
SUCH A HANDKERCHIEF-- I AM SURE IT WAS YOUR WIFE'S--DID I TODAY SEE CASSIO WIPE HIS BEARD WITH.
DAMN HER, LEWD MINX! O, DAMN HER!

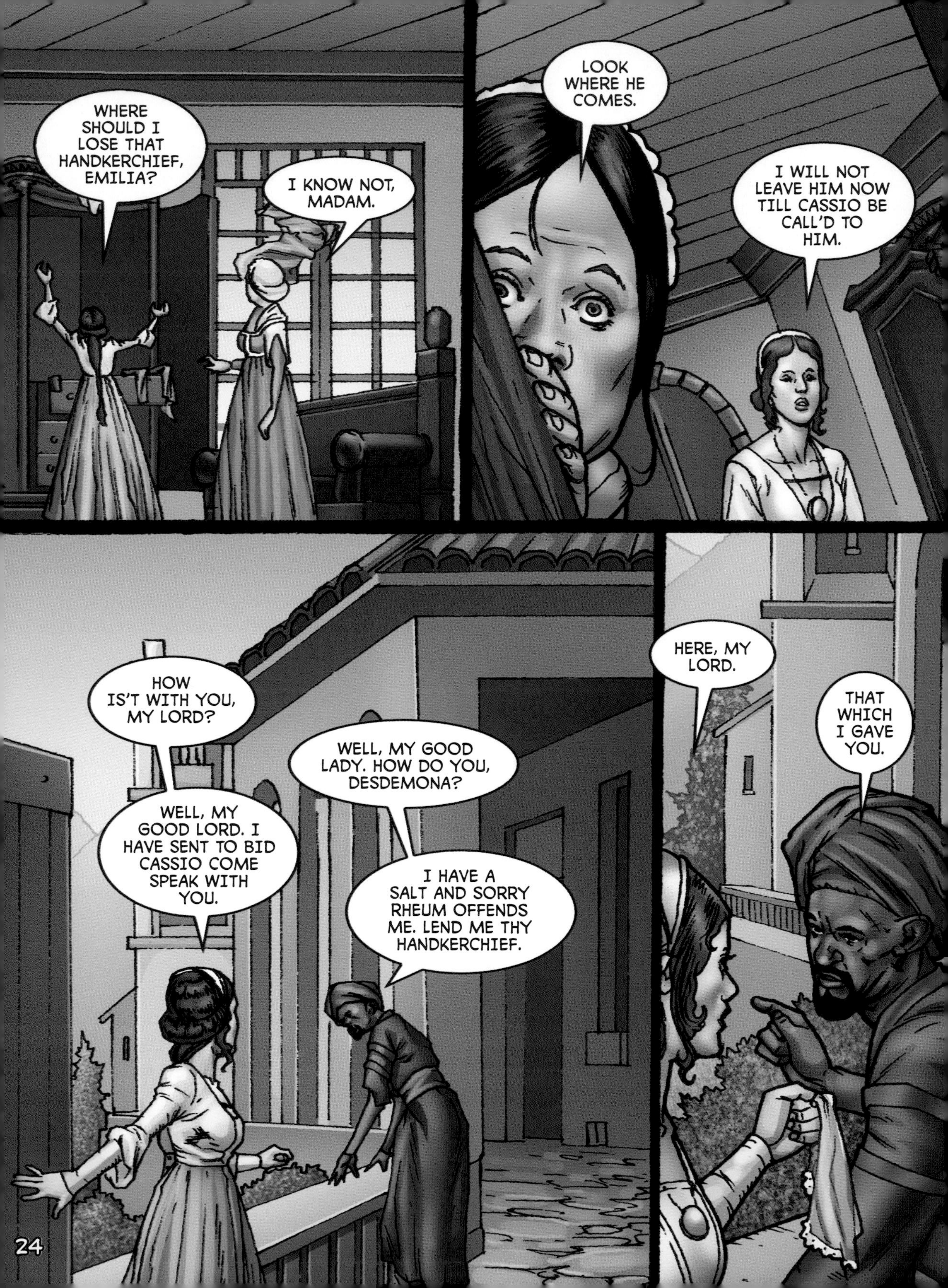
WHERE SHOULD I LOSE THAT HANDKERCHIEF, EMILIA?
I KNOW NOT, MADAM.
LOOK WHERE HE COMES.
I WILL NOT LEAVE HIM NOW TILL CASSIO BE CALL'D TO HIM.
HOW IS'T WITH YOU, MY LORD?
WELL, MY GOOD LADY. HOW DO YOU, DESDEMONA?
WELL, MY GOOD LORD. I HAVE SENT TO BID CASSIO COME SPEAK WITH YOU.
I HAVE A SALT AND SORRY RHEUM OFFENDS ME. LEND ME THY HANDKERCHIEF.
HERE, MY LORD.
THAT WHICH I GAVE YOU.

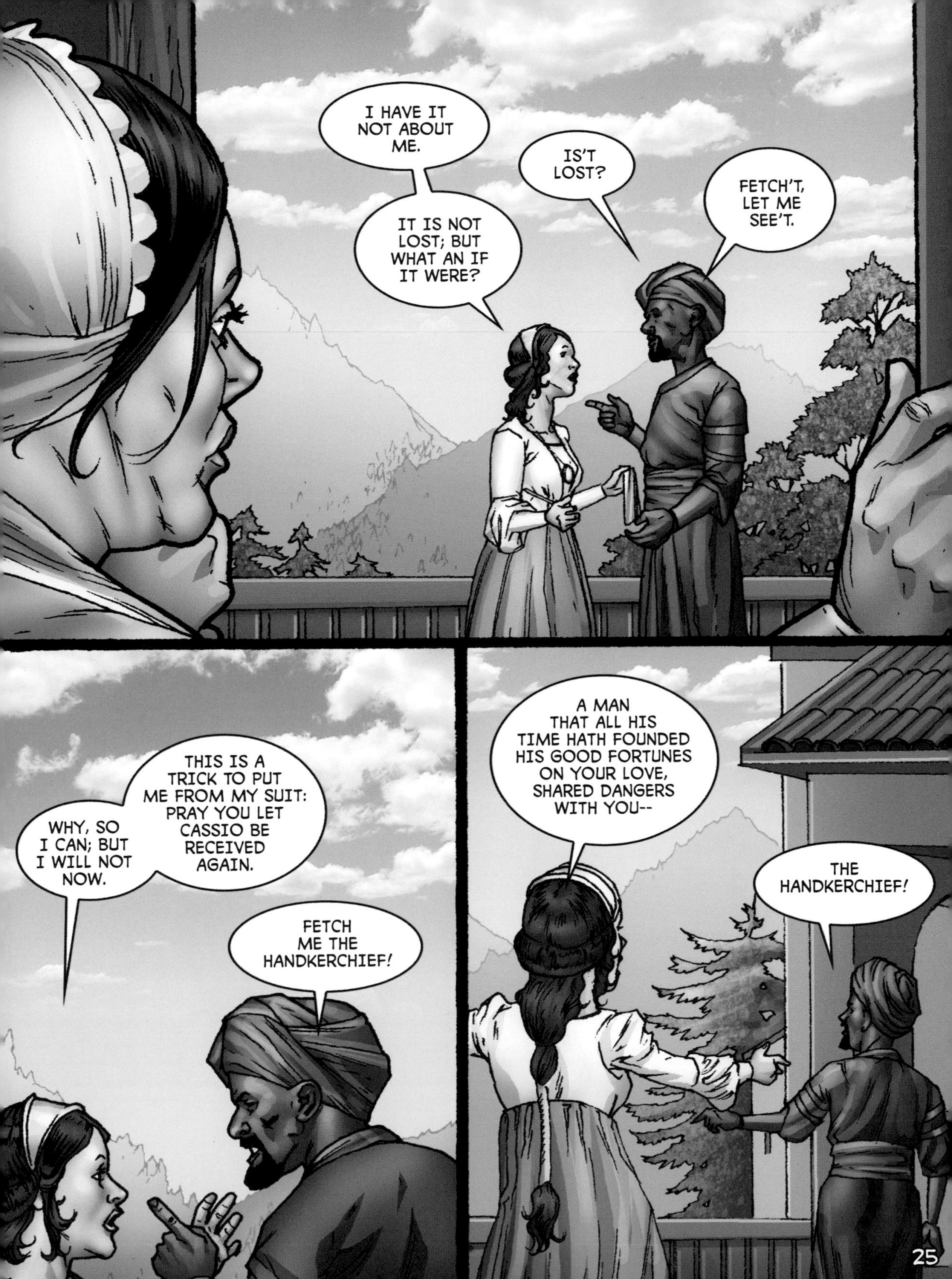
I HAVE IT NOT ABOUT ME.
IS'T LOST?
FETCH'T, LET ME SEE'T.
IT IS NOT LOST; BUT WHAT AN IF IT WERE?
WHY, SO I CAN; BUT I WILL NOT NOW.
THIS IS A TRICK TO PUT ME FROM MY SUIT: PRAY YOU LET CASSIO BE RECEIVED AGAIN.
FETCH ME THE HANDKERCHIEF!
A MAN THAT ALL HIS TIME HATH FOUNDED HIS GOOD FORTUNES ON YOUR LOVE, SHARED DANGERS WITH YOU--
THE HANDKERCHIEF!

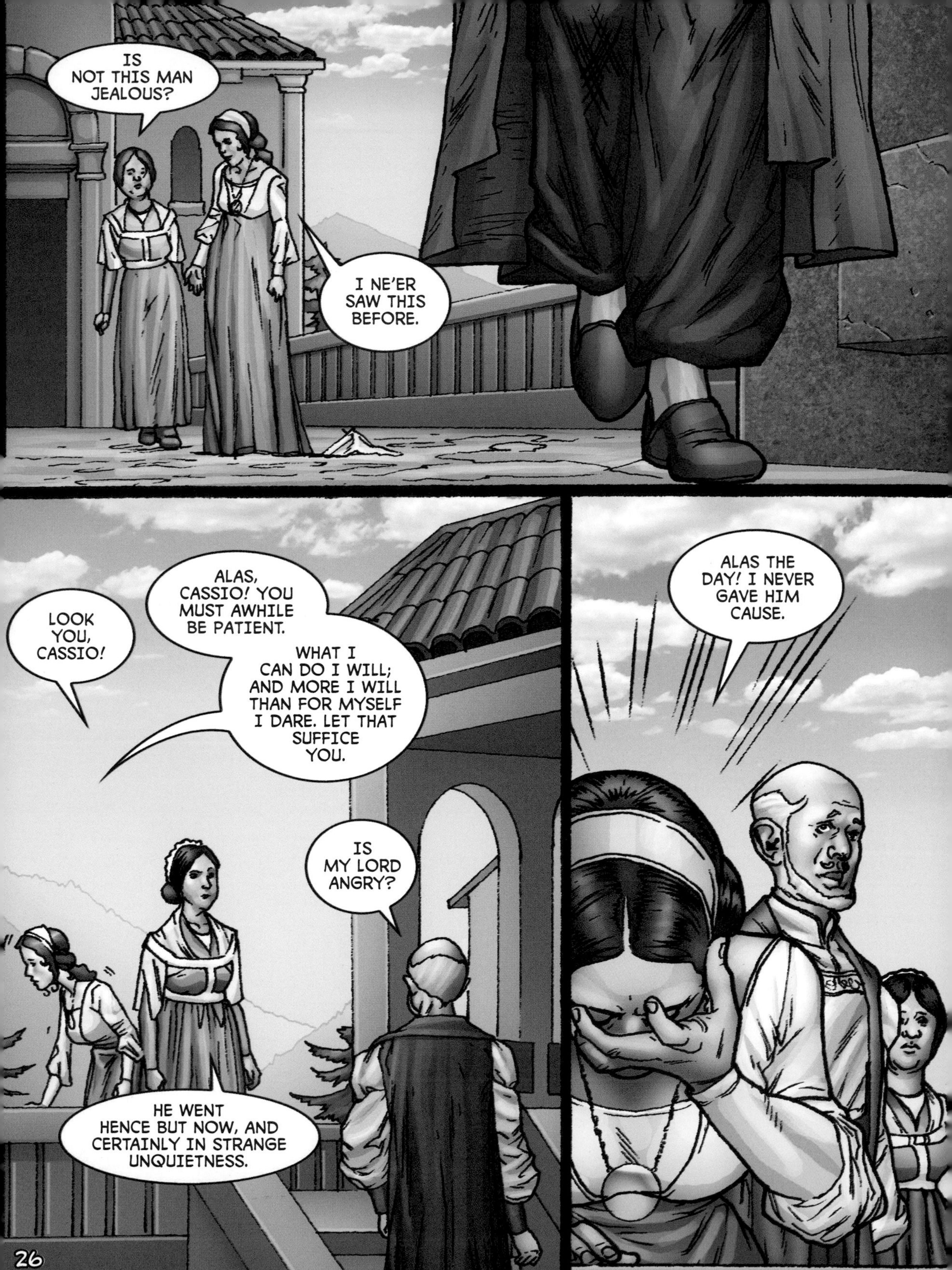
IS NOT THIS MAN JEALOUS?
I NE'ER SAW THIS BEFORE.
LOOK YOU, CASSIO!
ALAS, CASSIO! YOU MUST AWHILE BE PATIENT.
WHAT I CAN DO I WILL; AND MORE I WILL THAN FOR MYSELF I DARE. LET THAT SUFFICE YOU.
IS MY LORD ANGRY?
HE WENT HENCE BUT NOW, AND CERTAINLY IN STRANGE UNQUIETNESS.
ALAS THE DAY! I NEVER GAVE HIM CAUSE.

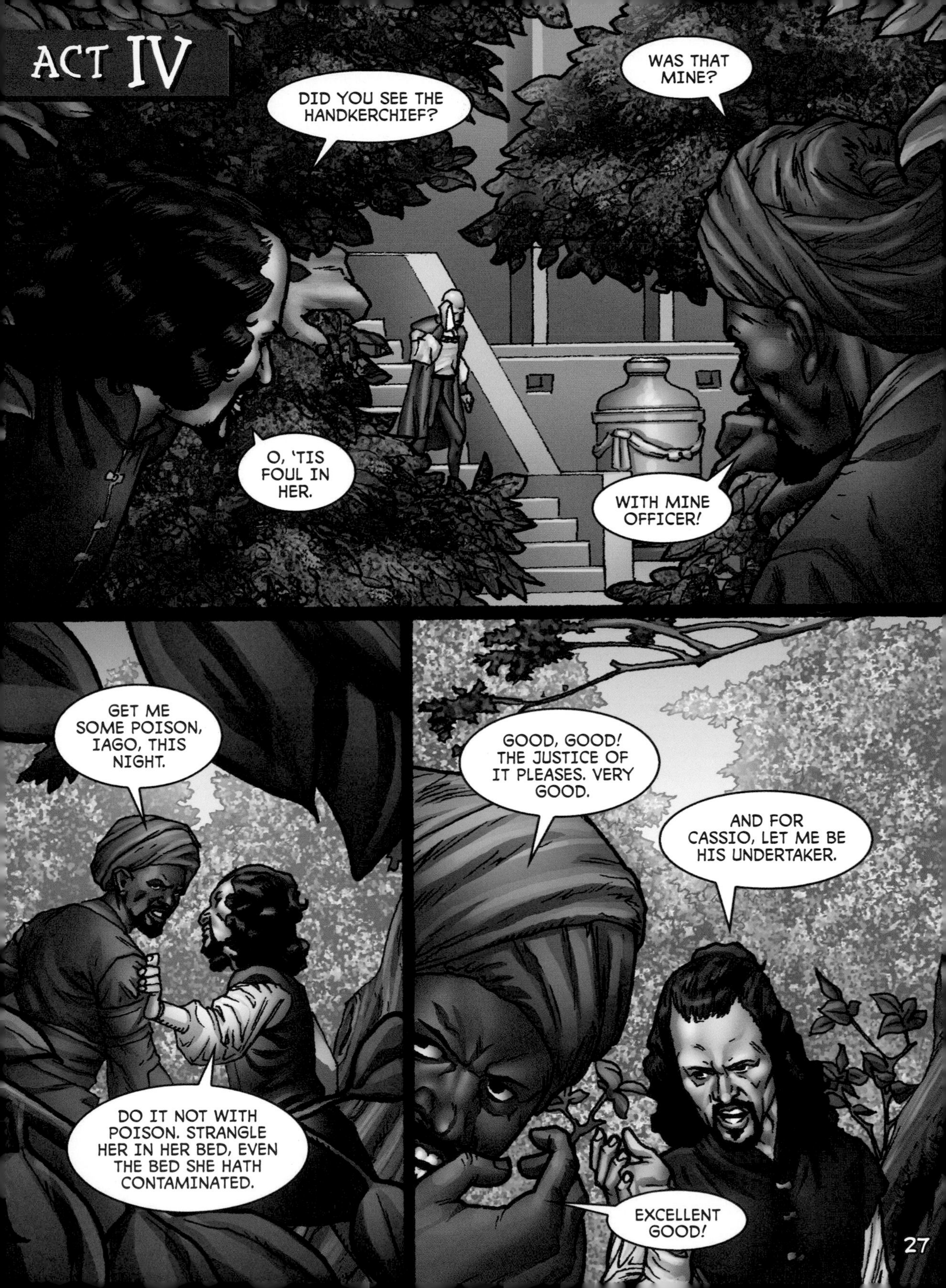
ACT IV
DID YOU SEE THE HANDKERCHIEF?
WAS THAT MINE?
O, 'TIS FOUL IN HER.
WITH MINE OFFICER!
GET ME SOME POISON, IAGO, THIS NIGHT.
DO IT NOT WITH POISON. STRANGLE HER IN HER BED, EVEN THE BED SHE HATH CONTAMINATED.
GOOD, GOOD! THE JUSTICE OF IT PLEASES. VERY GOOD.
AND FOR CASSIO, LET ME BE HIS UNDERTAKER.
EXCELLENT GOOD!

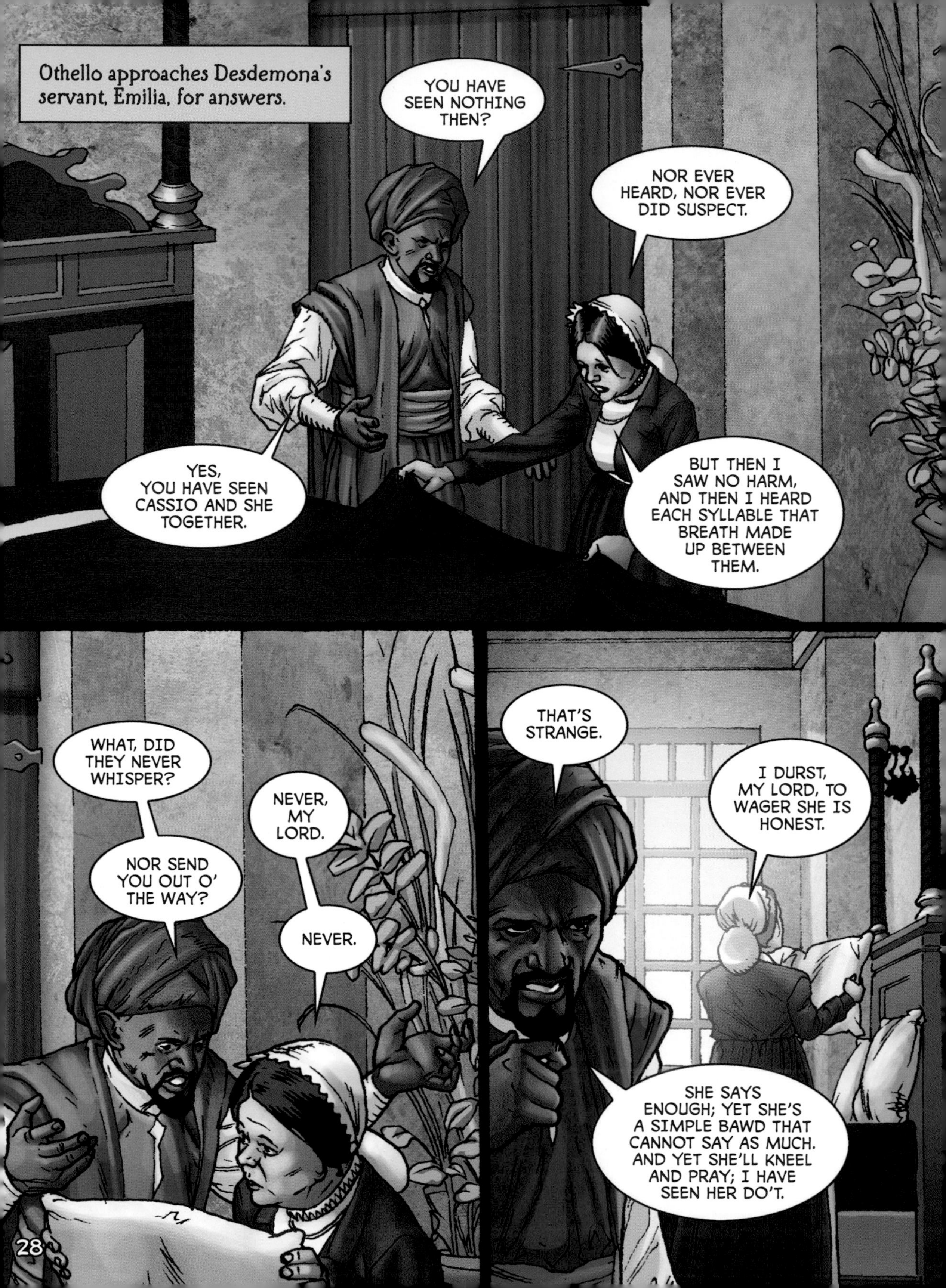
Othello approaches Desdemona's servant, Emilia, for answers.
YOU HAVE SEEN NOTHING THEN?
NOR EVER HEARD, NOR EVER DID SUSPECT.
YES, YOU HAVE SEEN CASSIO AND SHE TOGETHER.
BUT THEN I SAW NO HARM, AND THEN I HEARD EACH SYLLABLE THAT BREATH MADE UP BETWEEN THEM.
WHAT, DID THEY NEVER WHISPER?
NEVER, MY LORD.
NOR SEND YOU OUT O' THE WAY?
NEVER.
THAT'S STRANGE.
I DURST, MY LORD, TO WAGER SHE IS HONEST.
SHE SAYS ENOUGH; YET SHE'S A SIMPLE BAWD THAT CANNOT SAY AS MUCH. AND YET SHE'LL KNEEL AND PRAY; I HAVE SEEN HER DO'T.

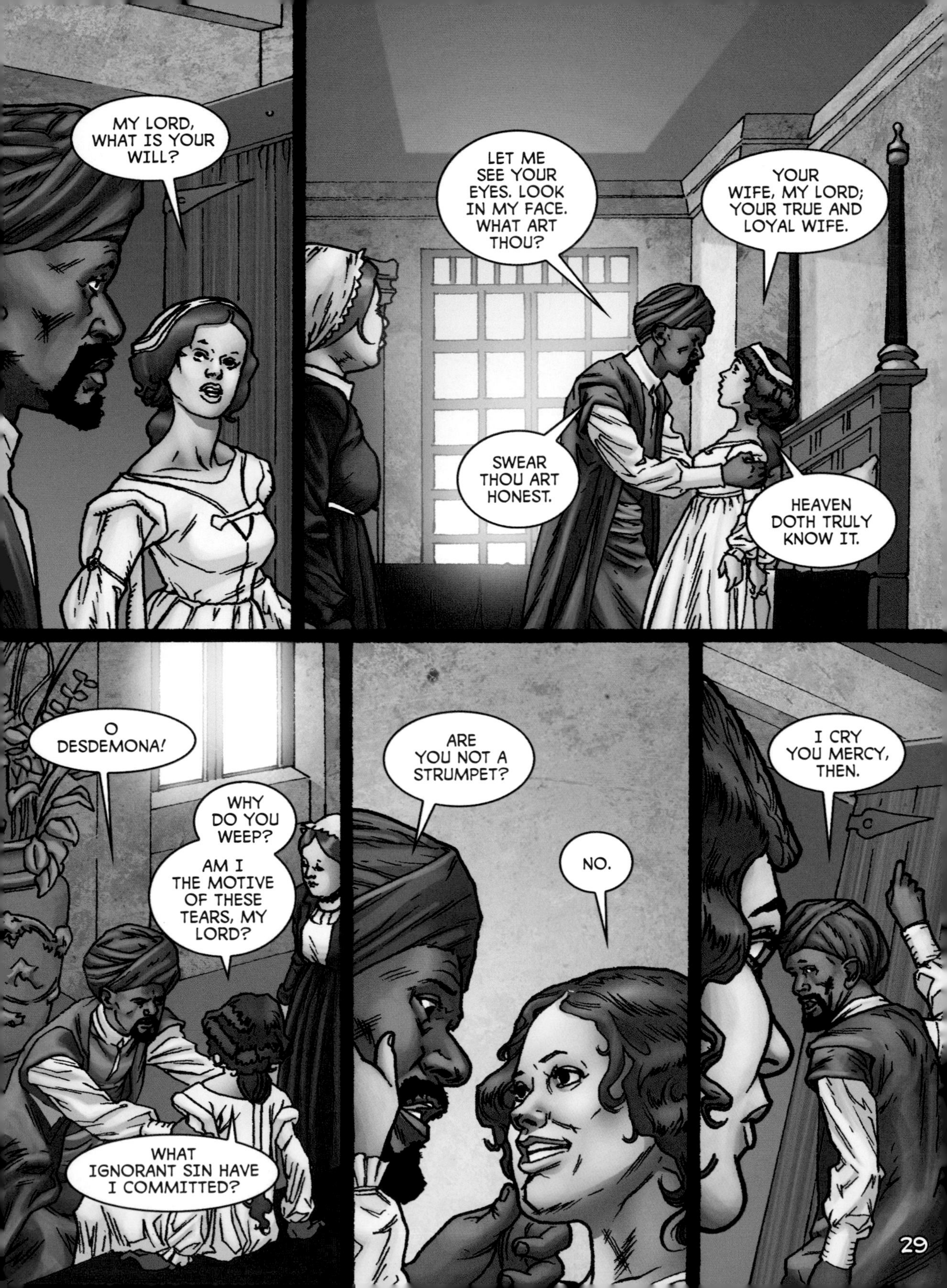
MY LORD, WHAT IS YOUR WILL?
LET ME SEE YOUR EYES. LOOK IN MY FACE. WHAT ART THOU?
YOUR WIFE, MY LORD; YOUR TRUE AND LOYAL WIFE.
SWEAR THOU ART HONEST.
HEAVEN DOTH TRULY KNOW IT.
O DESDEMONA!
WHY DO YOU WEEP?
AM I THE MOTIVE OF THESE TEARS, MY LORD?
WHAT IGNORANT SIN HAVE I COMMITTED?
ARE YOU NOT A STRUMPET?
NO.
I CRY YOU MERCY, THEN.

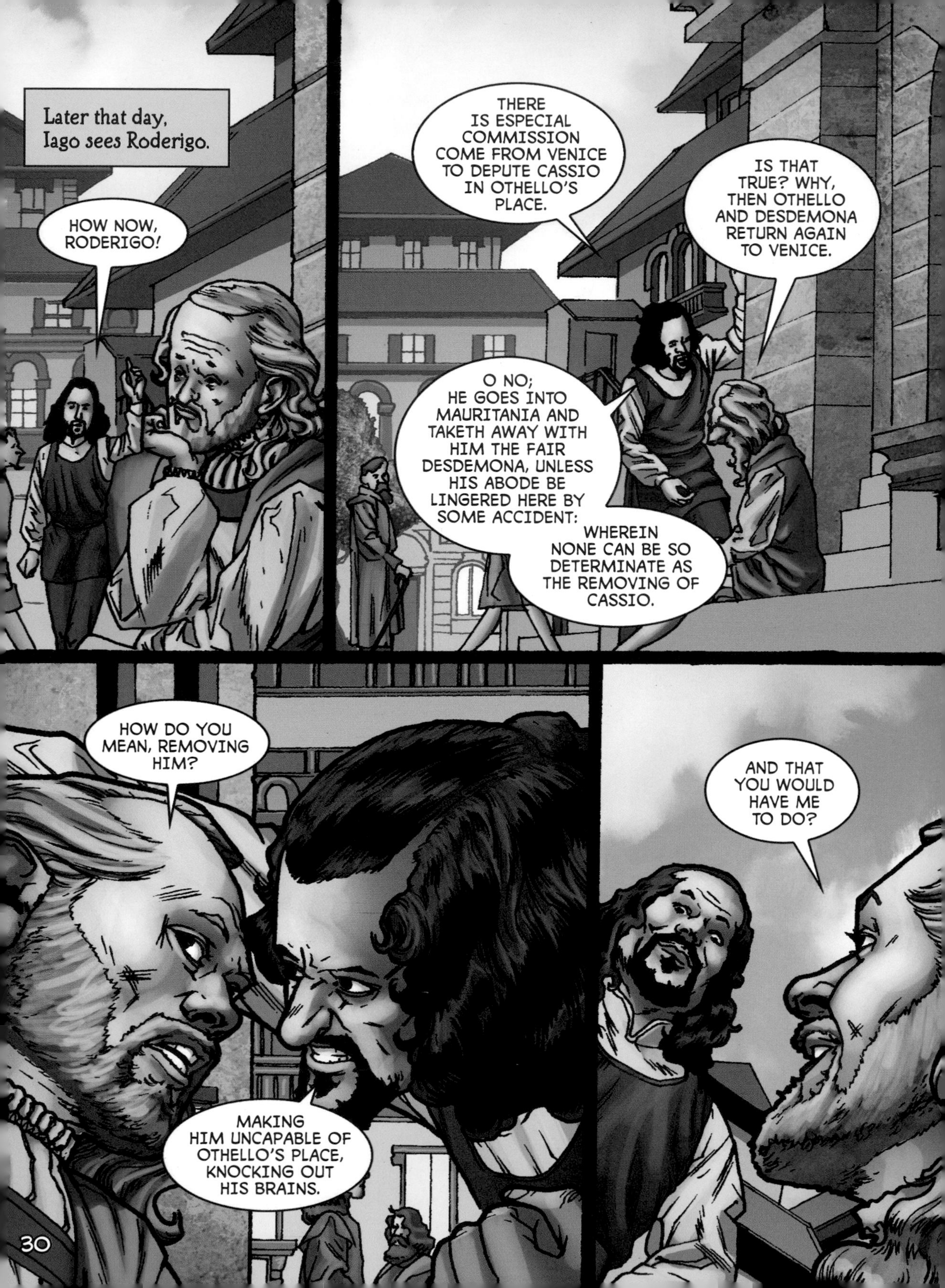

Later that day, Iago sees Roderigo.
HOW NOW, RODERIGO!
THERE IS ESPECIAL COMMISSION COME FROM VENICE TO DEPUTE CASSIO IN OTHELLO'S PLACE.
IS THAT TRUE? WHY, THEN OTHELLO AND DESDEMONA RETURN AGAIN TO VENICE.
O NO; HE GOES INTO MAURITANIA AND TAKETH AWAY WITH HIM THE FAIR DESDEMONA, UNLESS HIS ABODE BE LINGERED HERE BY SOME ACCIDENT:
WHEREIN NONE CAN BE SO DETERMINATE AS THE REMOVING OF CASSIO.
HOW DO YOU MEAN, REMOVING HIM?
MAKING HIM UNCAPABLE OF OTHELLO'S PLACE, KNOCKING OUT HIS BRAINS.
AND THAT YOU WOULD HAVE ME TO DO?

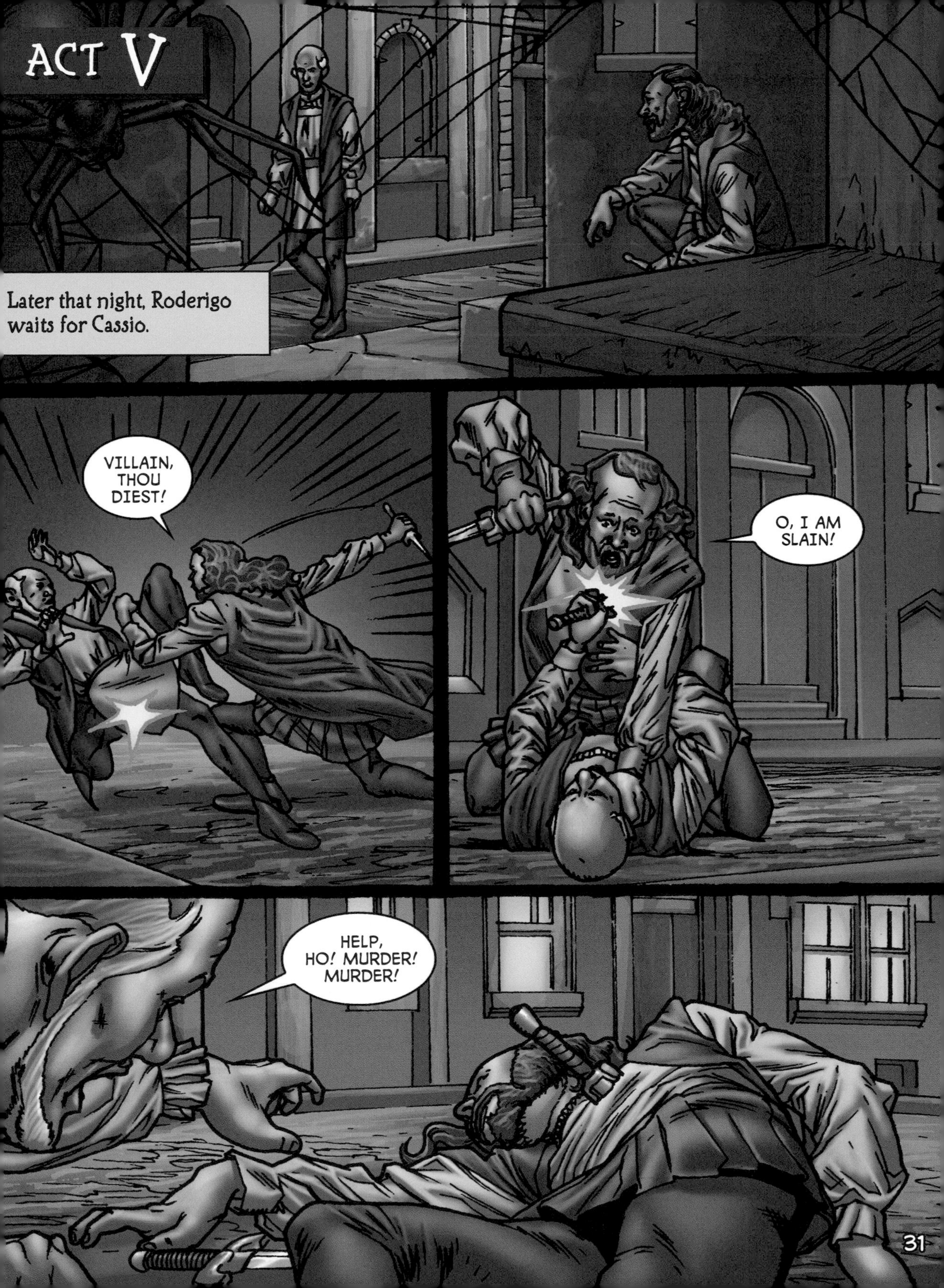
ACT V
Later that night, Roderigo waits for Cassio.
VILLAIN, THOU DIEST!
O, I AM SLAIN!
HELP, HO! MURDER! MURDER!

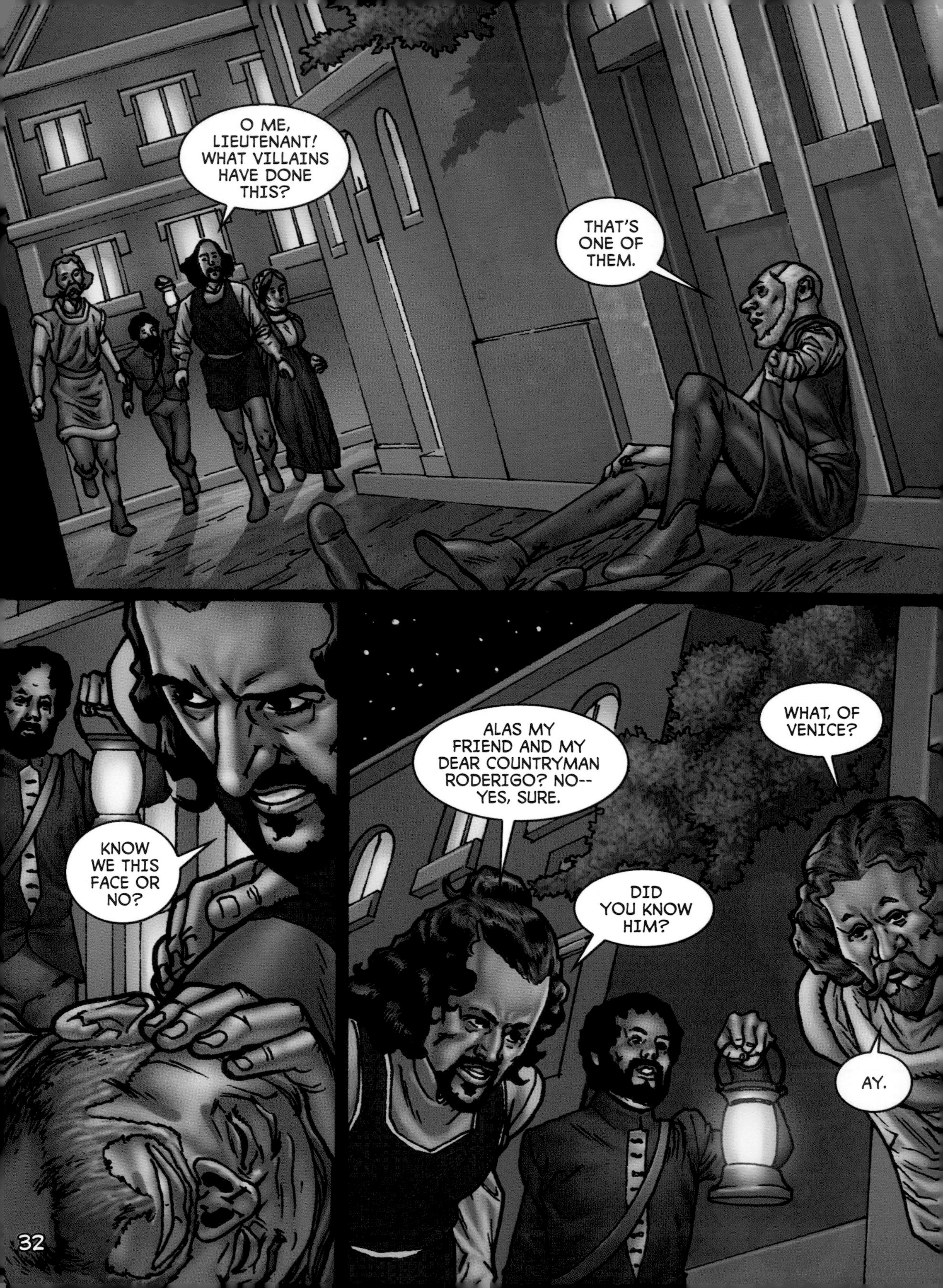
O ME, LIEUTENANT! WHAT VILLAINS HAVE DONE THIS?
THAT'S ONE OF THEM.
KNOW WE THIS FACE OR NO?
ALAS MY FRIEND AND MY DEAR COUNTRYMAN RODERIGO? NO-- YES, SURE.
WHAT, OF VENICE?
DID YOU KNOW HIM?
AY.

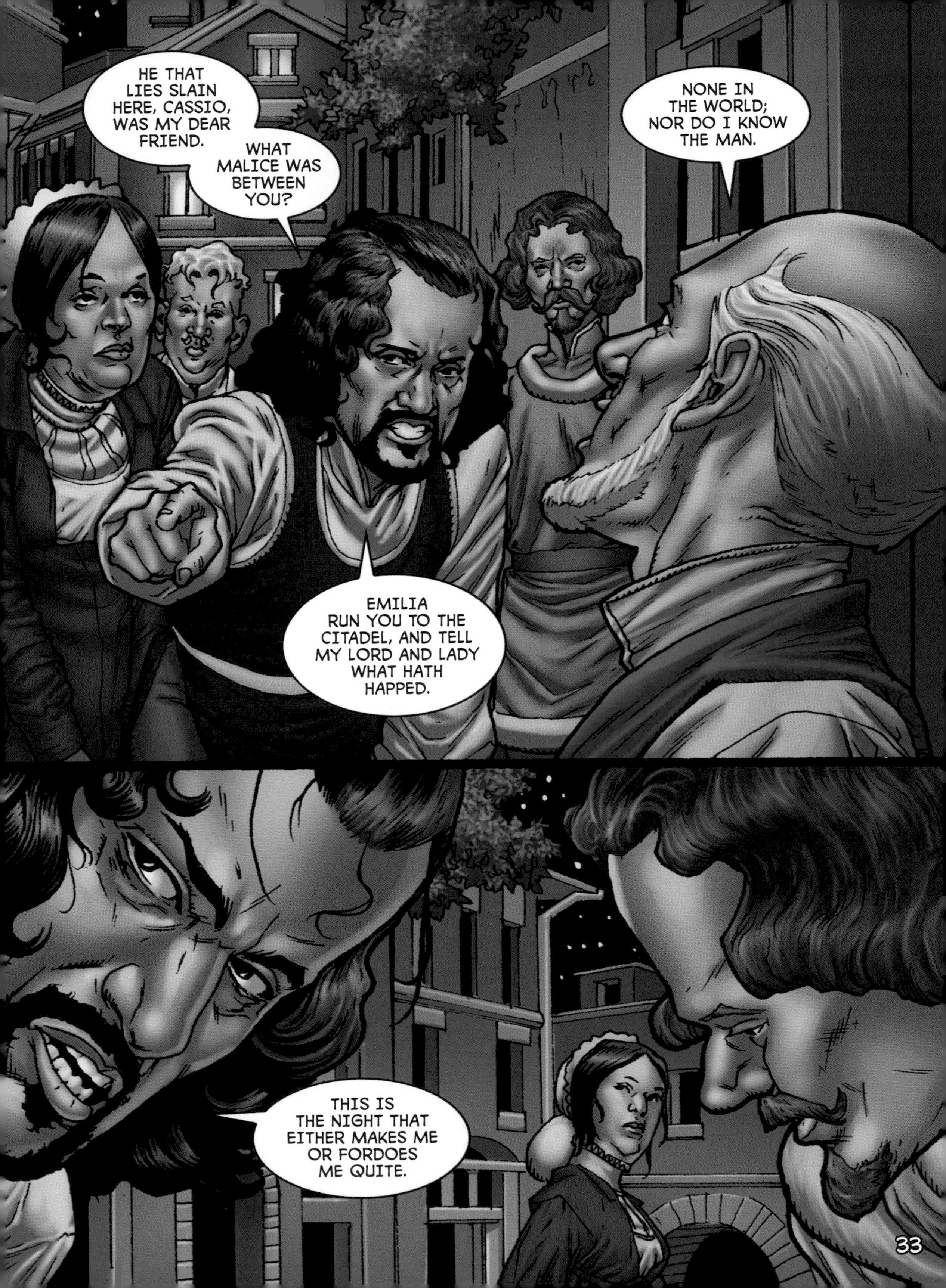

HE THAT LIES SLAIN HERE, CASSIO, WAS MY DEAR FRIEND.
WHAT MALICE WAS BETWEEN YOU?
NONE IN THE WORLD; NOR DO I KNOW THE MAN.
EMILIA RUN YOU TO THE CITADEL, AND TELL MY LORD AND LADY WHAT HATH HAPPED.
THIS IS THE NIGHT THAT EITHER MAKES ME OR FORDOES ME QUITE.

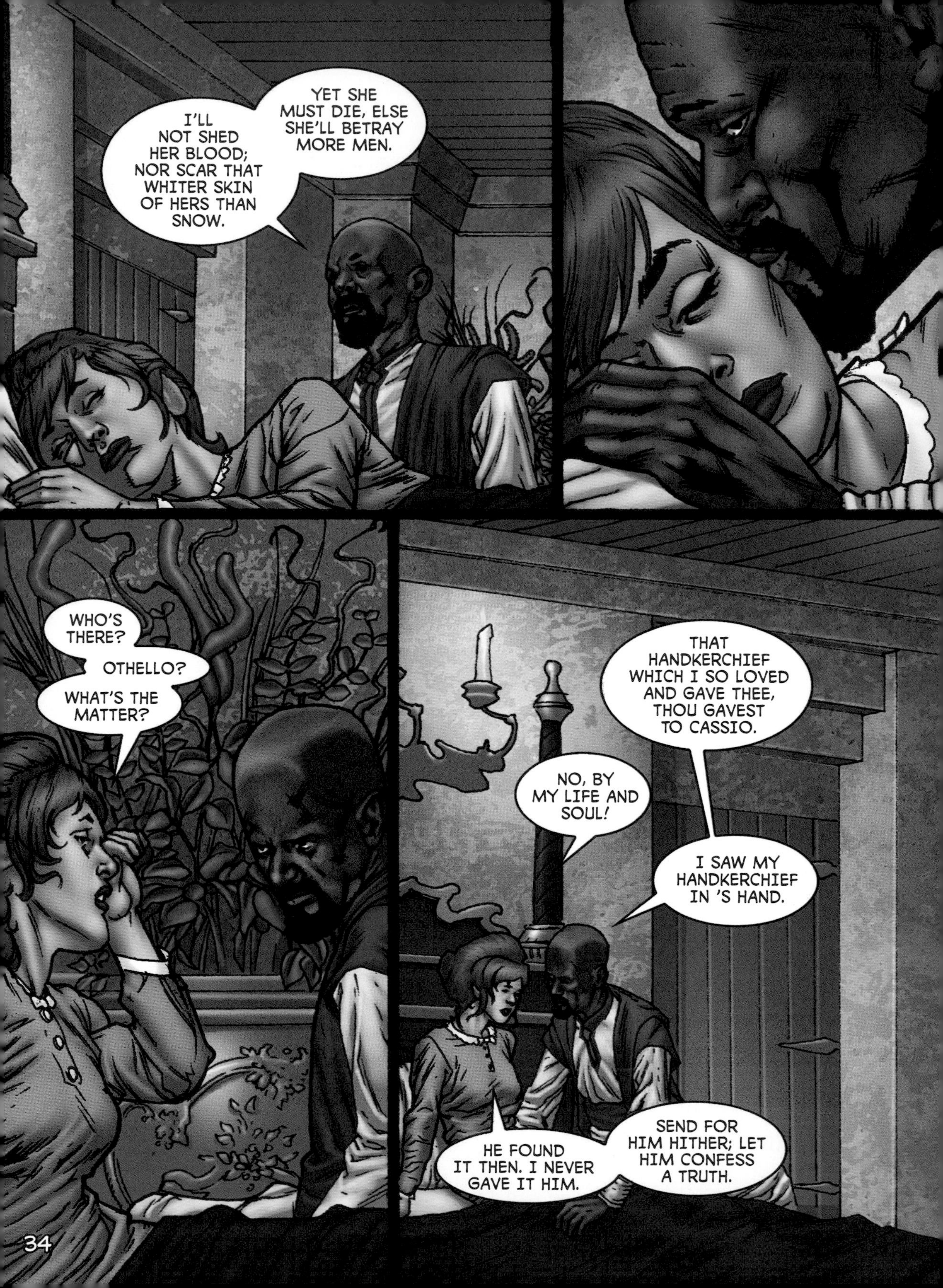
I'LL NOT SHED HER BLOOD; NOR SCAR THAT WHITER SKIN OF HERS THAN SNOW.
YET SHE MUST DIE, ELSE SHE'LL BETRAY MORE MEN.
WHO'S THERE?
OTHELLO?
WHAT'S THE MATTER?
THAT HANDKERCHIEF WHICH I SO LOVED AND GAVE THEE, THOU GAVEST TO CASSIO.
NO, BY MY LIFE AND SOUL!
I SAW MY HANDKERCHIEF IN 'S HAND.
HE FOUND IT THEN. I NEVER GAVE IT HIM.
SEND FOR HIM HITHER; LET HIM CONFESS A TRUTH.

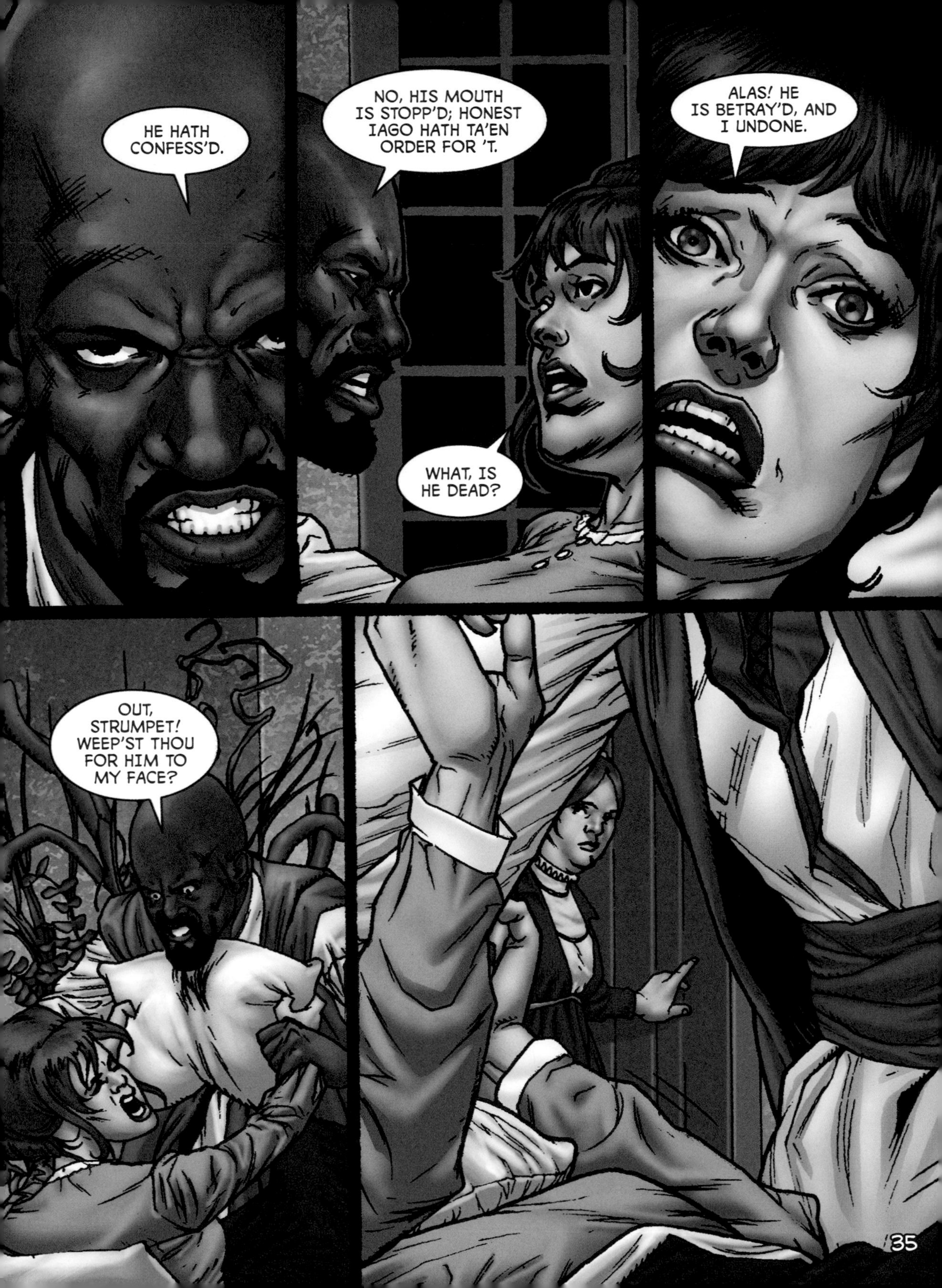
HE HATH CONFESS'D.
NO, HIS MOUTH IS STOPP'D; HONEST IAGO HATH TA'EN ORDER FOR 'T.
WHAT, IS HE DEAD?
ALAS! HE IS BETRAY'D, AND I UNDONE.
OUT, STRUMPET! WEEP'ST THOU FOR HIM TO MY FACE?

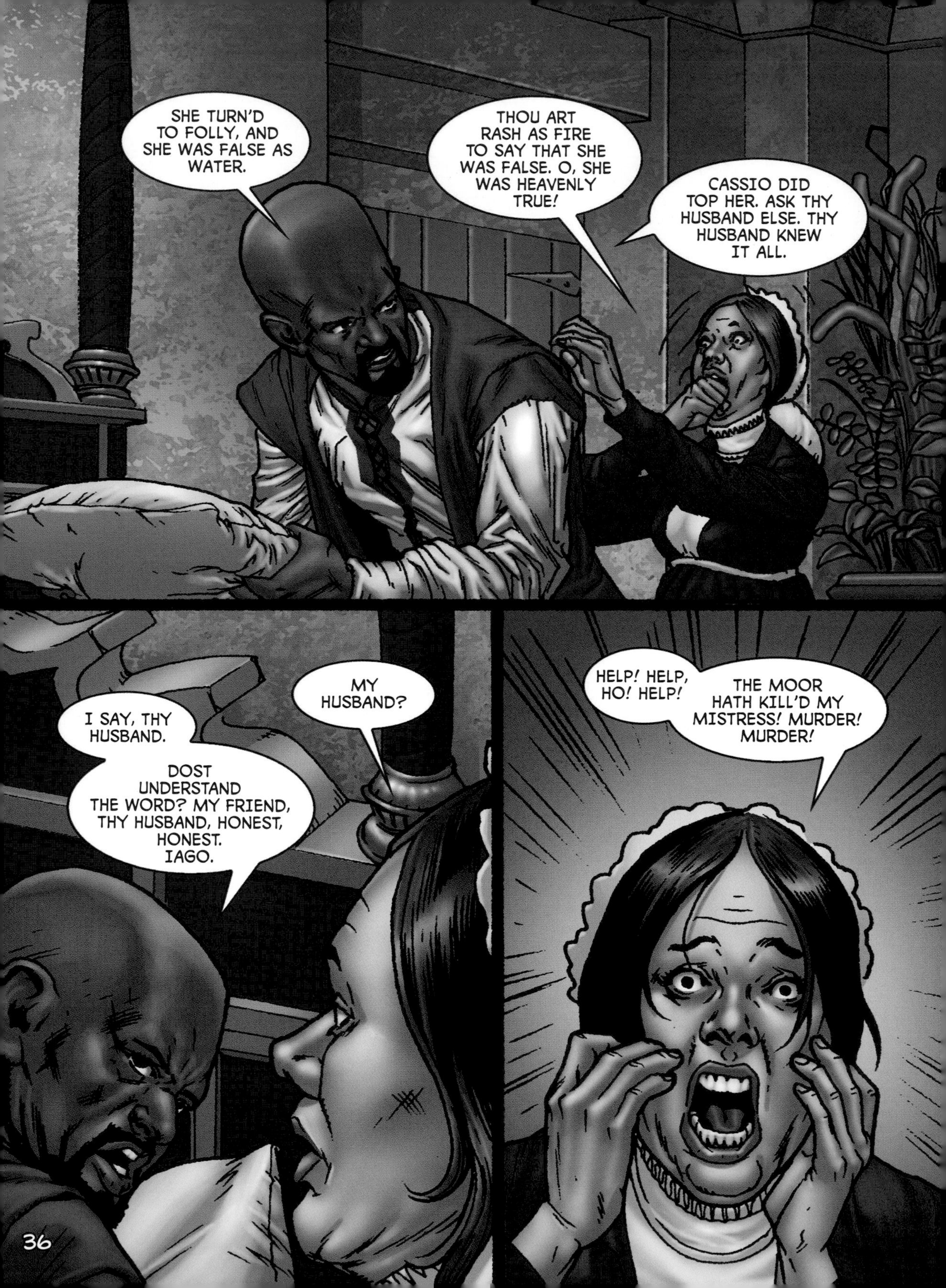

SHE TURN'D TO FOLLY, AND SHE WAS FALSE AS WATER.
THOU ART RASH AS FIRE TO SAY THAT SHE WAS FALSE. O, SHE WAS HEAVENLY TRUE!
CASSIO DID TOP HER. ASK THY HUSBAND ELSE. THY HUSBAND KNEW IT ALL.
MY HUSBAND?
I SAY, THY HUSBAND.
DOST UNDERSTAND THE WORD? MY FRIEND, THY HUSBAND, HONEST, HONEST. IAGO.
HELP! HELP, HO! HELP!
THE MOOR HATH KILL'D MY MISTRESS! MURDER! MURDER!

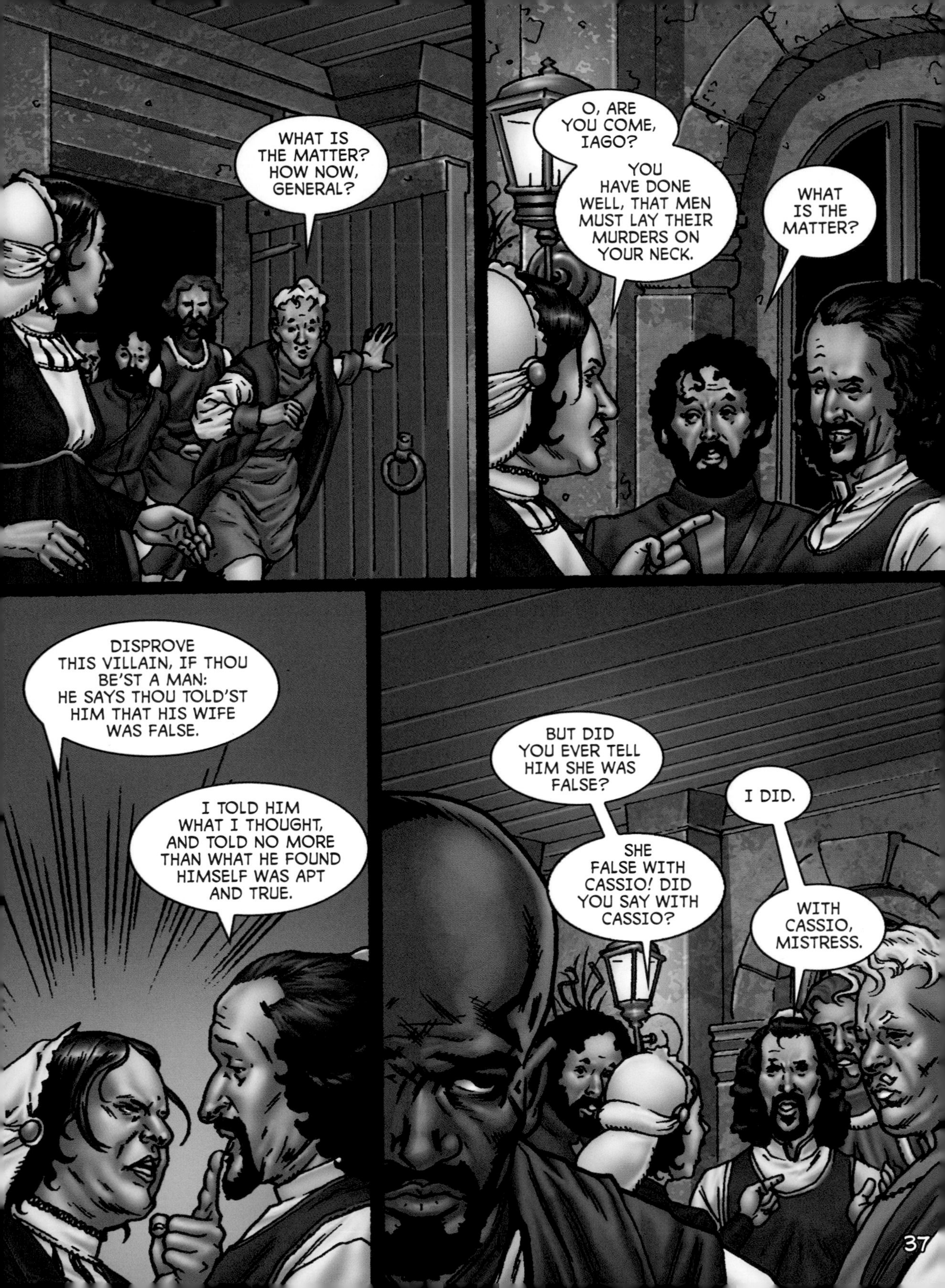

WHAT IS THE MATTER? HOW NOW, GENERAL?
O, ARE YOU COME, IAGO?
YOU HAVE DONE WELL, THAT MEN MUST LAY THEIR MURDERS ON YOUR NECK.
WHAT IS THE MATTER?
DISPROVE THIS VILLAIN, IF THOU BE'ST A MAN: HE SAYS THOU TOLD'ST HIM THAT HIS WIFE WAS FALSE.
I TOLD HIM WHAT I THOUGHT, AND TOLD NO MORE THAN WHAT HE FOUND HIMSELF WAS APT AND TRUE.
BUT DID YOU EVER TELL HIM SHE WAS FALSE?
I DID.
SHE FALSE WITH CASSIO! DID YOU SAY WITH CASSIO?
WITH CASSIO, MISTRESS.

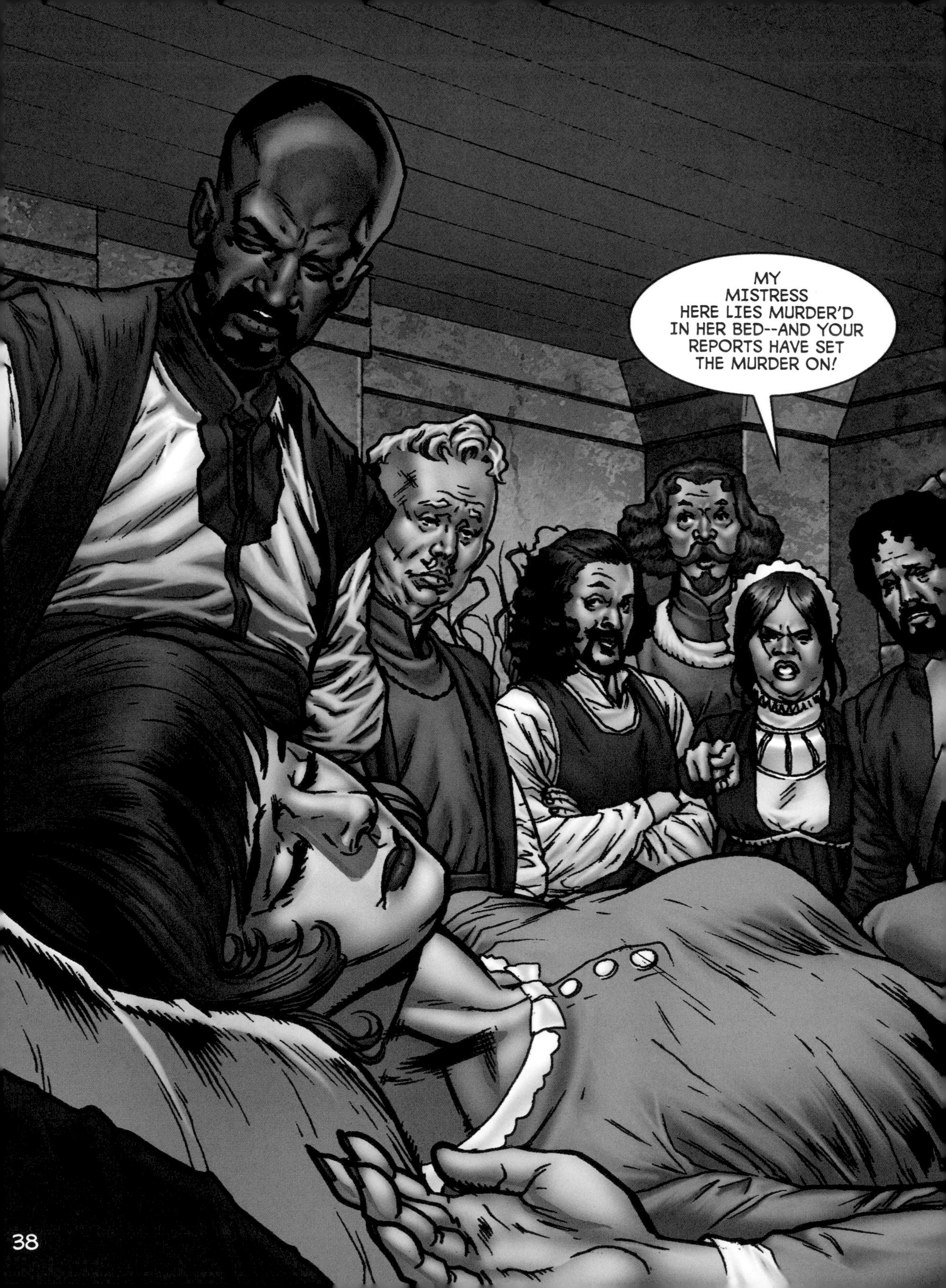
MY MISTRESS HERE LIES MURDER'D IN HER BED--AND YOUR REPORTS HAVE SET THE MURDER ON!

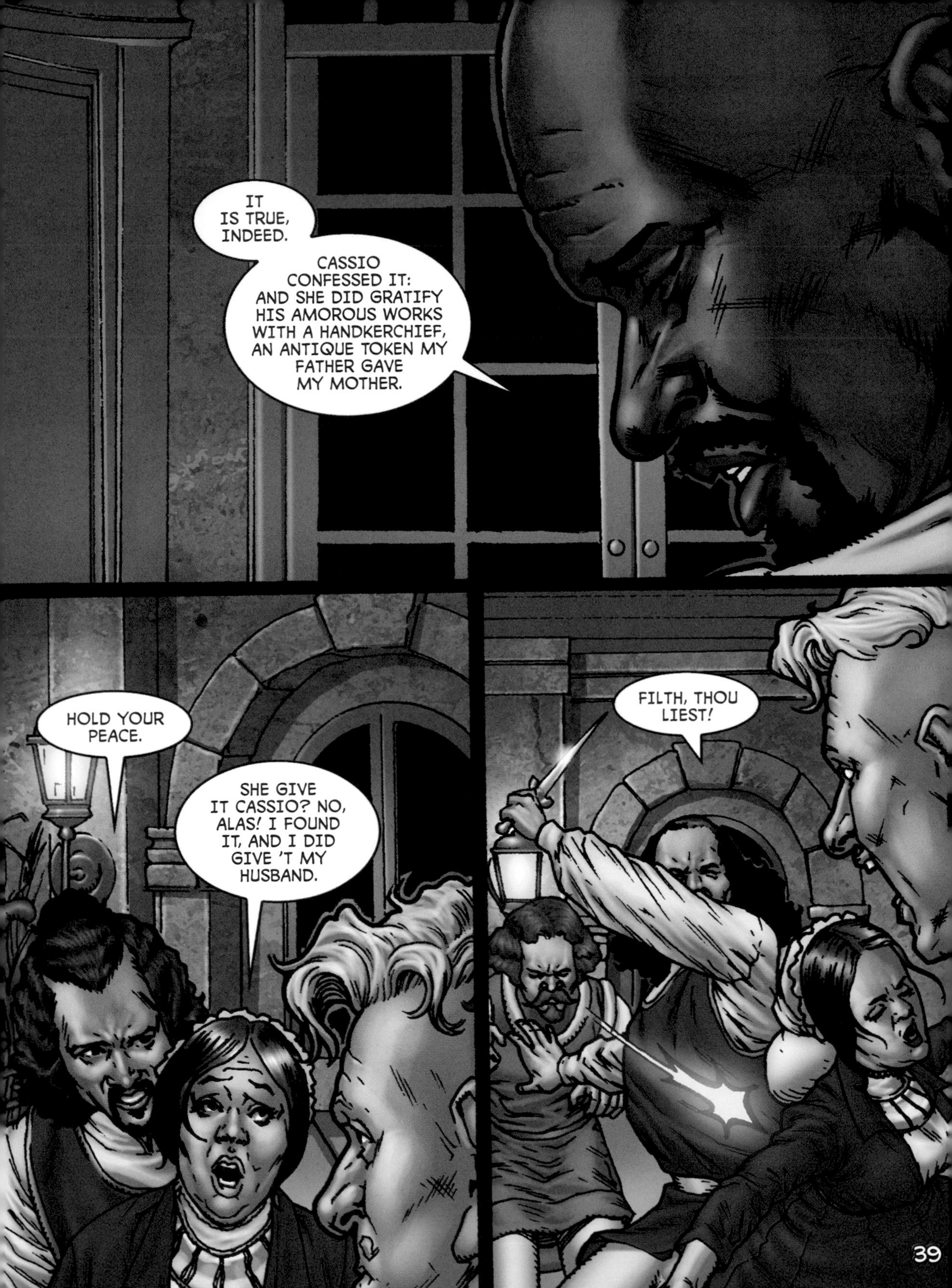
IT IS TRUE, INDEED.
CASSIO CONFESSED IT: AND SHE DID GRATIFY HIS AMOROUS WORKS WITH A HANDKERCHIEF, AN ANTIQUE TOKEN MY FATHER GAVE MY MOTHER.
HOLD YOUR PEACE.
SHE GIVE IT CASSIO? NO, ALAS! I FOUND IT, AND I DID GIVE 'T MY HUSBAND.
FILTH, THOU LIEST!

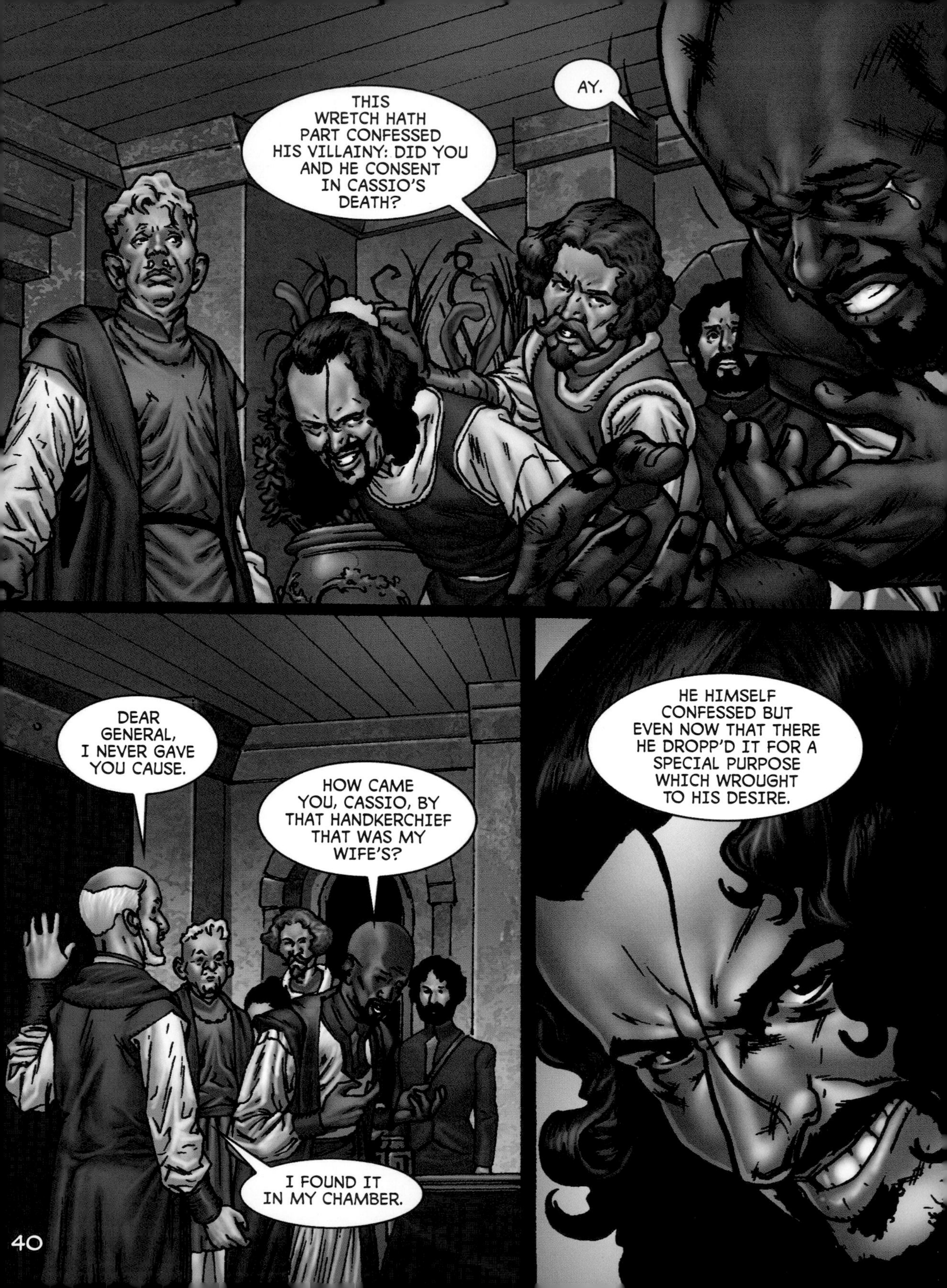
THIS WRETCH HATH PART CONFESSED HIS VILLAINY: DID YOU AND HE CONSENT IN CASSIO'S DEATH?
AY.
DEAR GENERAL, I NEVER GAVE YOU CAUSE.
HOW CAME YOU, CASSIO, BY THAT HANDKERCHIEF THAT WAS MY WIFE'S?
I FOUND IT IN MY CHAMBER.
HE HIMSELF CONFESSED BUT EVEN NOW THAT THERE HE DROPP'D IT FOR A SPECIAL PURPOSE WHICH WROUGHT TO HIS DESIRE.

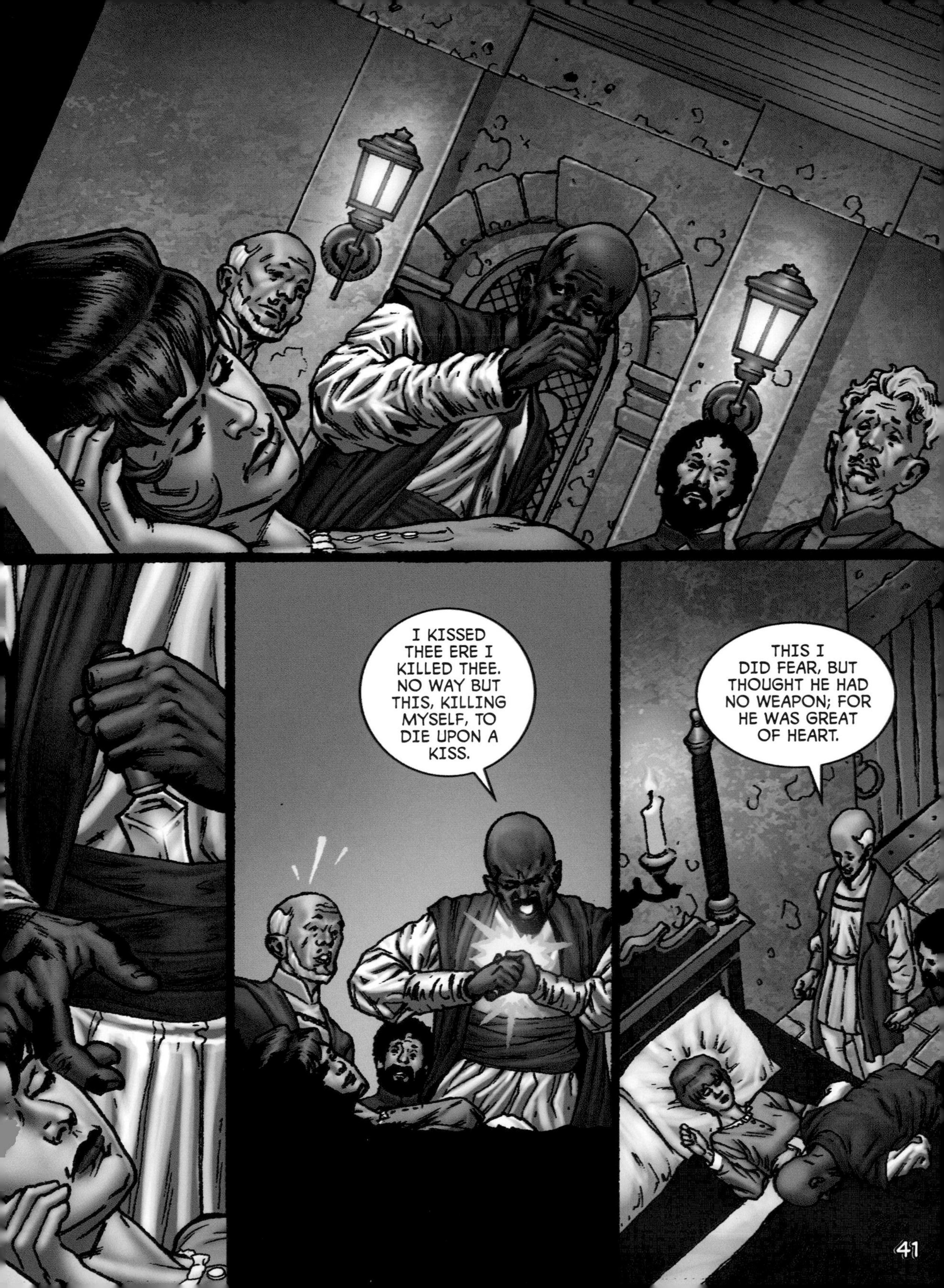
I KISSED THEE ERE I KILLED THEE. NO WAY BUT THIS, KILLING MYSELF, TO DIE UPON A KISS.
THIS I DID FEAR, BUT THOUGHT HE HAD NO WEAPON; FOR HE WAS GREAT OF HEART.

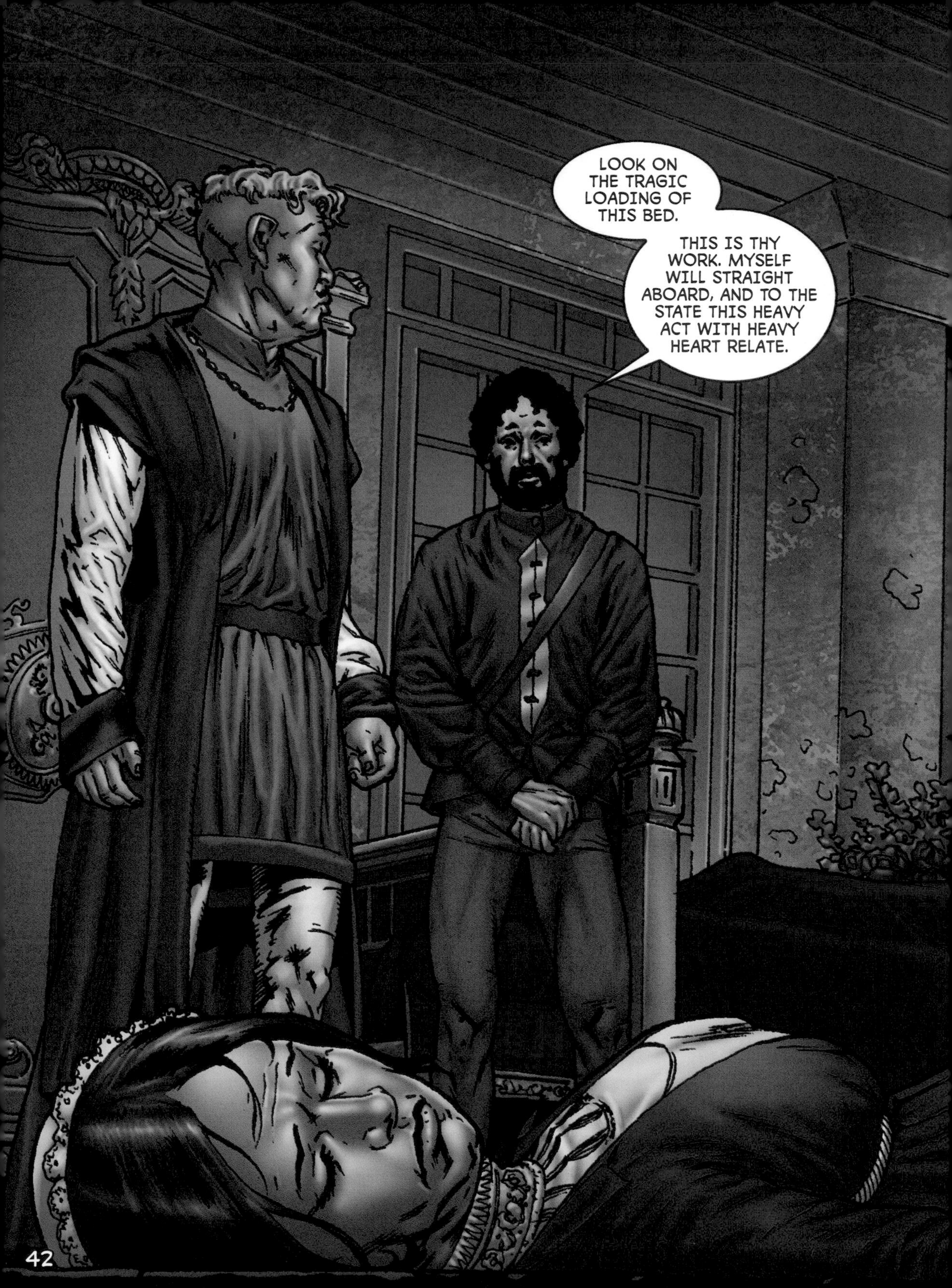
LOOK ON THE TRAGIC LOADING OF THIS BED.
THIS IS THY WORK. MYSELF WILL STRAIGHT ABOARD, AND TO THE STATE THIS HEAVY ACT WITH HEAVY HEART RELATE.

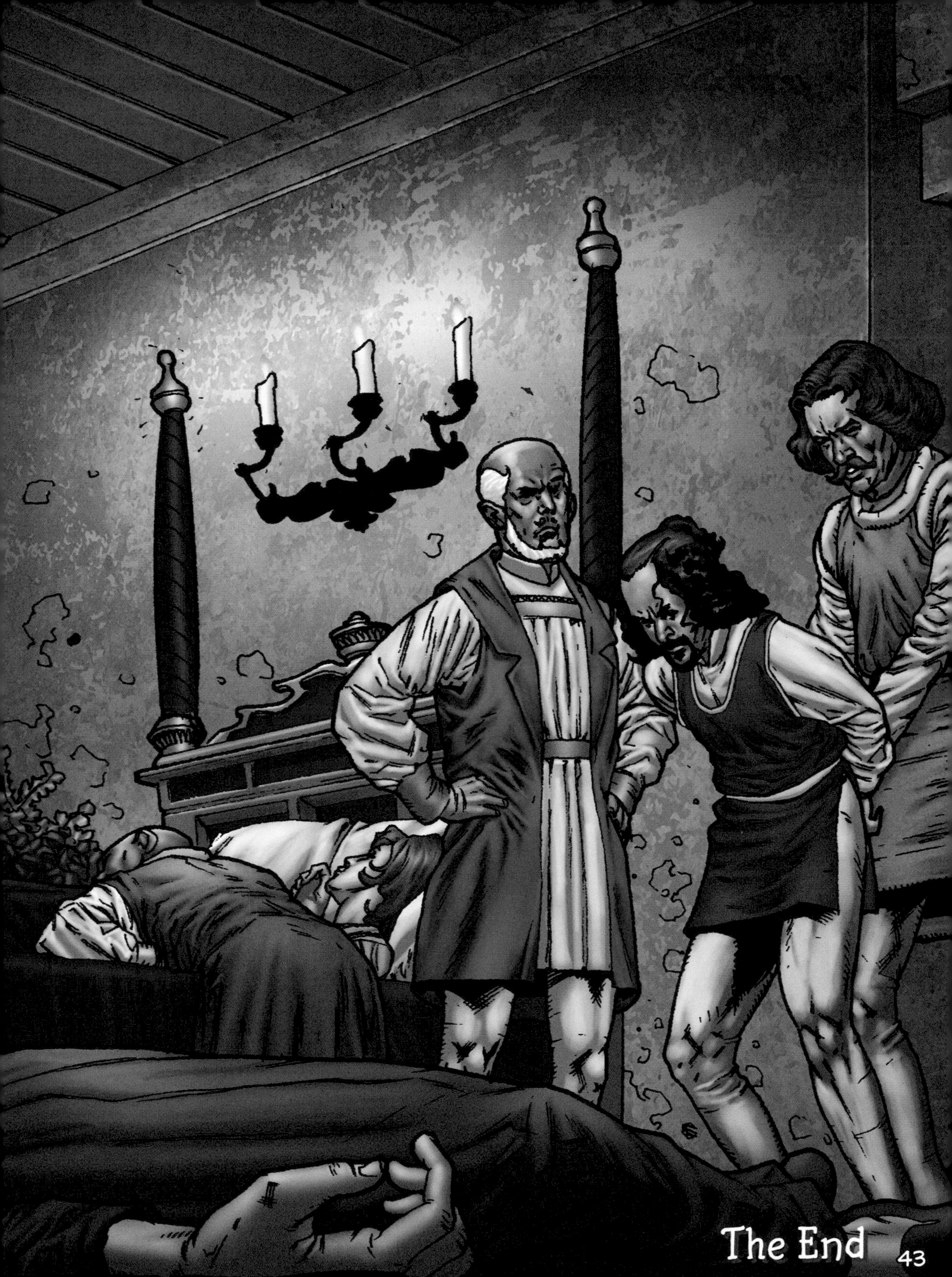
The End

Discussion Questions

1. Iago wants revenge after Othello passes him over and promotes Cassio. What other reasons might Iago have for his actions?

2. Desdemona's handkerchief symbolizes different things to different people in the play. What does it symbolize for Desdemona? For Othello? For Iago?

3. Othello, who is in love with Desdemona, moves to wanting to kill her in only one act. He ultimately commits the deed. What are the key events that caused this rapid decline?

4. Othello is Black. In what ways does Othello's race affect the way others perceive him? How does it affect how he sees himself?

5. The emotions of love, hate, fear, and jealousy drive the action in the play. How do these emotions inform Othello's actions? How do they inform Iago's?

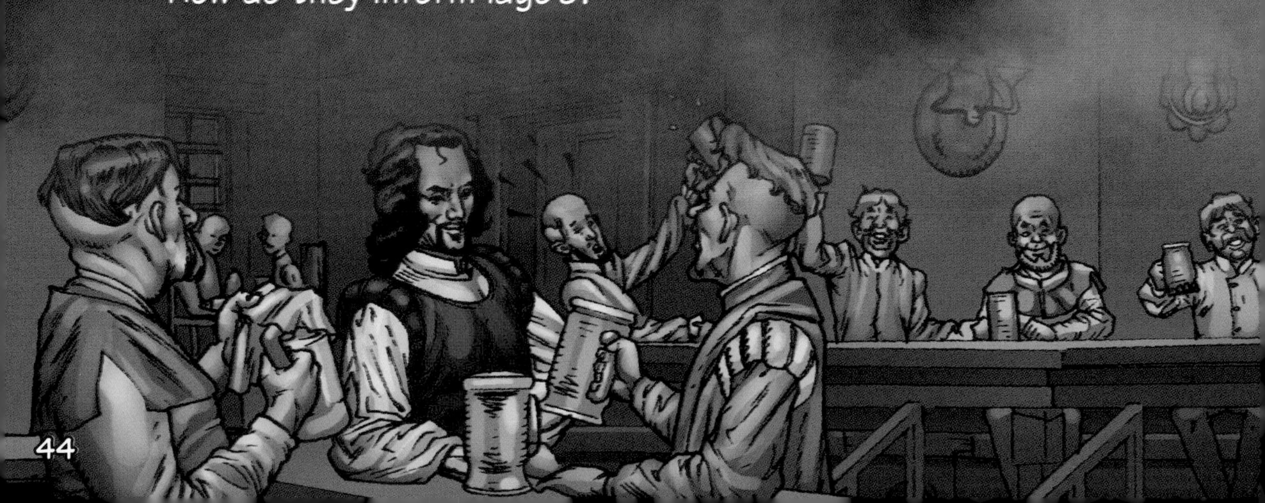

Fun Facts

- Othello was inspired by the Italian story Hecatommithi.

- Ira Aldridge was the first Black actor to play Othello in the 1830s.

- England's first known stage actress was Margaret Hughes, who played Desdemona in 1660.

- Iago has 31 percent of the lines in the play, with more than 1,000 lines. This is more lines than the title character Othello.

- "Honest" is said about 50 times in the play, and almost half the time it's describing Iago.

- A Danish layer cake, made of macaroon, custard cream, and chocolate, is named after the play.

About Shakespeare

Records show William Shakespeare was baptized at Holy Trinity Church in Stratford-upon-Avon, England, on April 26, 1564. There were few birth records at the time, but Shakespeare's birthday is commonly recognized as April 23 of that year. His middle-class parents were John Shakespeare and Mary Arden. John was a tradesman who made gloves.

William most likely went to grammar school, but he did not go to university. He married Anne Hathaway in 1582, and they had three children: Susanna and twins Hamnet and Judith. Shakespeare was in London by 1592 working as an actor and playwright. He began to stand out for his writing. Later in his career, he partly owned the Globe Theater in London, and he was known throughout England.

To mark Shakespeare and his colleagues' success, King James I (reigned 1603–1625) named their theater company King's Men—a great honor. Shakespeare returned to Stratford in his retirement and died April 23, 1616. He was 52 years old.

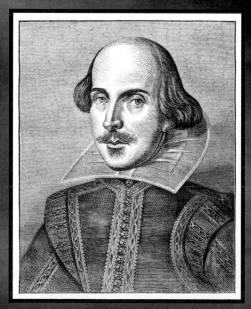

Famous Phrases

*I will wear my heart upon my sleeve for daws to peck at.
I am not what I am.*

*Reputation, reputation, reputation! O, I have lost my
reputation!*

*O, beware, my lord, of jealousy; it is the green-eyed monster,
which doth mock the meat that it feeds on.*

Glossary

citadel - a city's fortress.

cuckold - a man whose wife is
unfaithful.

durst - dare.

haste-posthaste - hurry with great
speed.

hearted - deeply felt in one's heart.

mazzard - head.

minx - wanton.

Moor – a member of a North African
Arab group.

mutualities - exchanges.

ocular - based on what is seen.

odd-even - midnight, the time when
it is difficult to tell one day from
the next.

pestilence - a dangerous disease.

prithee - a way to make a request.

rheum - watering of the eyes.

rogue - a dishonest or worthless
person.

Additional Works by Shakespeare

Romeo and Juliet (1594–96)

A Midsummer Night's Dream (1595–96)

The Merchant of Venice (1596–97)

Much Ado About Nothing (1598–99)

Hamlet (1599–1601)

Twelfth Night (1600–02)

Othello (1603–04)

King Lear (1605–06)

Macbeth (1606–07)

The Tempest (1610–11)

- *Bold titles are available in this set of Shakespeare Illustrated Classics.*

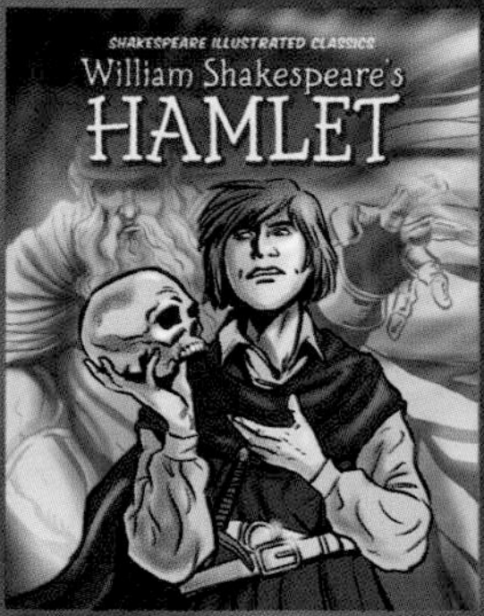
SHAKESPEARE ILLUSTRATED CLASSICS
William Shakespeare's
HAMLET

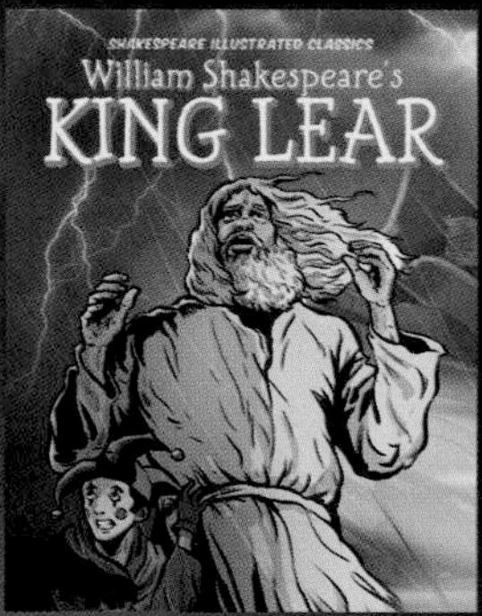
SHAKESPEARE ILLUSTRATED CLASSICS
William Shakespeare's
KING LEAR

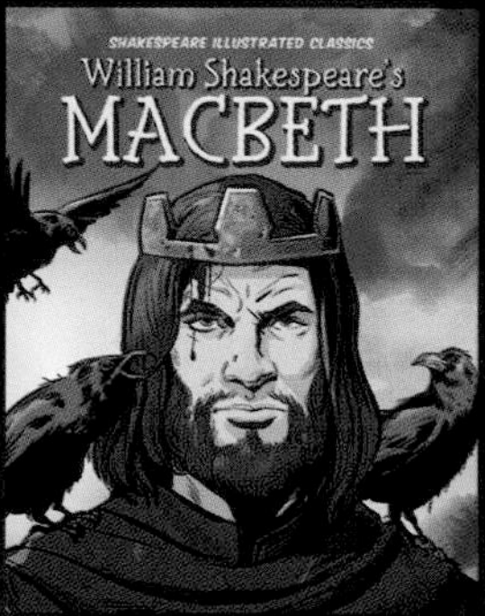
SHAKESPEARE ILLUSTRATED CLASSICS
William Shakespeare's
MACBETH

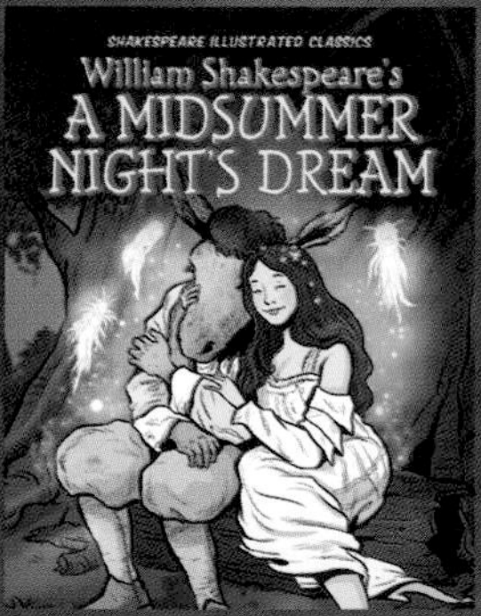
SHAKESPEARE ILLUSTRATED CLASSICS
William Shakespeare's
A MIDSUMMER NIGHT'S DREAM

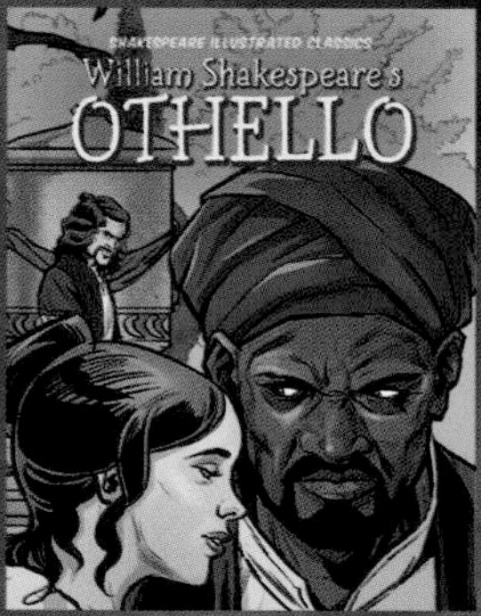
SHAKESPEARE ILLUSTRATED CLASSICS
William Shakespeare's
OTHELLO

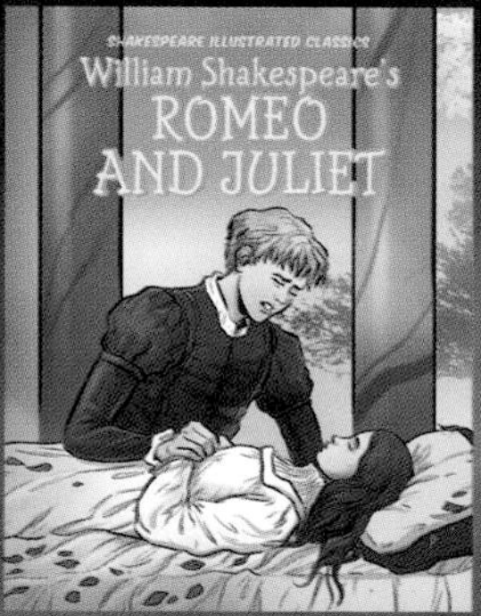
SHAKESPEARE ILLUSTRATED CLASSICS
William Shakespeare's
ROMEO AND JULIET